Phoneme Media
1551 Colorado Blvd., Ste. 201
Los Angeles, CA 90041

First Edition, 2016

Translation © 2016 Christopher Schaefer

Published by arrangement with Vents d'aileurs.

ISBN: 978-1-939419-62-0

This book is distributed by Publishers Group West.

Designed and typeset by Jaya Nicely
Cover art by Jaya Nicely

Phoneme Media is a nonprofit media company, a fiscally sponsored
project of PEN Center USA, dedicated to showcasing lesser heard
voices from around the world through the art of translation.

http://phoneme.media

Curious books for curious people.

ROLAND RUGERO

A NOVEL

TRANSLATED FROM THE FRENCH
BY CHRISTOPHER SCHAEFER

PHONEME
MEDIA
Los Angeles

...Warapfunywe,
Ntiwapfuye...

**You have been crumpled,
You haven't been taken**

Verse from the National Anthem of Burundi

To my mother, for all you have given me

To U.C., for all the adventures

I

Kahise gategura kazoza
The past presages the future

It's November, and the heavens are naked.

Ashamed, they try to tug a few clouds over to cover up under the merciless sun, which brings their nakedness unflinchingly to light.

Naked blue. Water blue. The color of Lake Tanganyika, that undulating plain to the West. Springs are scattered across the valleys surrounding Kanya. Not so long ago the water there was clear and crystalline, abundant. Now it is gone. A dry November.

Tucked among Hariho's many hills, Kanya has bravely weathered this dry season's sweltering onslaught, which invariably torments the region. It needs to breathe. And it waits for rain. A thirst for air and for humidity.

Kanya's hill is still draped in the eucalyptus of the National Forest. Dry, prickly leaves, countless, dense, and towering, spread over the earth. Without water, the sky has become spiteful.

Or rather, men have committed too many sins. It is God's punishment for this country's great evil.

An old woman is standing at the foot of the hill. She rests her age-worn cheek on a shepherd's crook. With it, she tends to a couple of skinny kids foraging in the pebbles and the weeds trying to find something to round out their scrawny bellies.

The earth's drought meets her eye. She understands: Times have changed.

In the past, the valleys were always green, the rain's absence offset by the murmur of many rivers flitting through the Hariho region.

Corn had its seasons. Millet and goosegrass. Peas as well. And wheat and cassava. In moments of hunger, there was always the banana tree. There was the green bean and its leaves. The sweet potato. Occasionally even the squash and its green, hairy tangle on every streambank. The granaries were stuffed to overflowing. There was enough to eat, to serve visitors, and to offer the passerby. Even the thief in the field was tolerated; the excess was there for the taking. It would have been a mark of shame for a family to go hungry, improbable as it was in those days so full of good cheer.

These thoughts swirled through her head. In those days her husband would gleefully haggle over a plump pig, a goat, or a cow. He kept his afternoons for relaxation, wrapped in his long overcoat that smelled of herbs and the land. After a day of hoeing, he had to rest. And rest, like work, is social.

The men drank. Excessively. A multitude of hands and lips grasping the straw each afternoon. It was a daily ritual to watch the banana wine dance at the bottom of a half-slit gourd. So many throats clamoring about the content and richness of *intangos*, those round and seductive vast clay vases! One rarely said that a man was "drunk." No, he was "beer-sated." Drinking was a meal that furnished endless afternoon arguments and evening deliberations. In those days, men were certain of their futures: repeated moments of repetition.

With several blows from her crook, the one-eyed old woman beats the kids' hindquarters like tambourines until they inch forward. She understands that her animals are blinded by the paucity of the fare on offer from the land.

Queen of the blind. How times are tough!

In those days, upon completing the field work each evening, the wife would immediately leave to prepare the meal for her husband and children. Hearths were kindled among the tufts of banana plantations, the plots of the Harahais. The last arrivals ran to get water. And then tremors of the *Umugabo*'s imminent return. The man. He who inspired fear and desire with his virile presence.

The Harahais would go to bed early in those times of little worry. Around eight in the evening, or sometimes an hour earlier, they curled up in protection against the piercing cold that invaded sleeping quarters, only to lie awake under the moonlight. After the evening gatherings, their clothing, the walls, and even their children's dreams were perfumed by stories and riddles around the cheerful fire. They had much, ate little, and went to bed early. Hunger did not scare them.

Because, for these people, the one who runs is assumed guilty of one thing or another. Slow seasons mark life's moments. One season peacefully leads into another, steady, slow, predictable and calm. Just as life itself is peace, regularity, and slowness. What is new surprises, astounds, and disconcerts.

They did not run from time; they knew it was always near them.

Through her left eye, the one-eyed old woman had seen close friends stray from this noble way of life. They said it was necessary to send their own to school! Time had protected her from such a grave course of action. The wife of a rich and prosperous man, she had insisted that her plentiful green fields not wither away for lack of hands on hoes, machetes, and curved billhooks. For lack of rolled-up sleeves! So her two sons had stayed on the hill: valiant, solid ramparts protecting the modest family's prosperity.

Her husband had died of old age. Time had carried him off. He was a husband, a man of peace, a man of the fields, and a beloved neighbor. A malicious saying labels noble souls as the most vulnerable, whereas, in truth, they are the ones who endure.

The one-eyed old woman also had four girls who were carried off by time. Four weddings had solidified the family's patrimony of goats and cattle. Her sons knew how to look after their father's legacy. At this their mother rejoiced, content yet resigned. Content with the good flow of business. Resigned that her own had to leave. Would her girls' husbands also be upstanding men like their father?

Life passed, and her left eye continued to function. It was long ago, during a sinister month of August, that the right one had suddenly stopped making out her path. She cried out for help. Her mother rushed up and rubbed a home-made liquor tonic through the still functional slits of her eyelids… But the sun still would not break through the whitish membrane that veiled her pupil. The young girl cried. Wept and sobbed! Time had been unjust to her. Life had dealt her this half-blindness when she was young, prudent, and lovely. And why? What had she done?

Now she knew life had given her a single eye to leisurely and safely enjoy the fruits that she had brought into the world. How pleasant the memory of those times was to her! Her only surprise had been that eye which had abandoned her so early. The rest had occurred in peace: time and humanity, the cycles of life, slowness and certainty. Objectives accomplished: a good marriage, her daughters married later on, her husband's fields still thriving…

And then came the war of '93, which threw everything into turmoil. The green fruits that life intended to bring to maturity were carried off. Men were torn apart, ripped to pieces by machetes, pierced by bullets, eaten away by poisonous death, and violated by the unspeakable. The war severed time from humanity in the Hariho way of life. It showed that time does change! It spurred men to the insanity of massacres. It made them see glory in the euphoria of violence. Then it sunk low, so low that it revealed—in the gasping throes of anguish—that in reality, life is a trilogy. A trilogy of humanity, time, and place.

The war managed to sever humanity from place. It was discovered with a certain dread that man has no place except through his history and culture. Violate those and it crumbles away. Man flees, to be ruled by nothing more than the growls of his own belly—of fear, and of hunger. Once again, he becomes a wandering beast that haunts the woods by day and by night.

The war had unmasked Burundi's countenance, thought the old woman. The war…She couldn't let it keep swirling through her old brain.

Incredibly powerful screams break out on the other side of the hill.

Responses in unison, in the harsh hues of the surrounding hamlets' drought, heat, and hunger.

Riven through the shouts, a rage to hold the guilty party responsible for all of this and for other misfortunes as well.

Unceasing: *"Fata, fata, fata!"*

In unison: "Seize him, seize him, seize him!"

The imperative becomes clear with the full unfolding of the cries: "Grab the bastard, the thief! Grab that dog! Grab that…"

A gust of wind whips the cloth that had been carefully wound around the one-eyed old woman's tough body. The

Nkunda kurya yariye igifyera kimumena amatama
The glutton ate the snail and it made his cheeks explode

With her left eye, the one-eyed woman tries to make out the pack of pursuers.

With the other eye, her bad one, she searches her thoughts. Tears escape them both. It is hard work with sweat trickling down. One eye makes out reality, and the other seeks the explanation for its harshness. One sees, and the other deliberates. The old woman's comprehension in either case is muddled.

By the time the sun's luminous fingers came to rest on Hariho's fields, his neck was already sore. Undeniably, nights are cold in these parts.

This morning he had come down to this trickle of water to rest, like a mosquito sated after a night pumping blood from the depths of tired and world-weary veins. He was calm, his mind flush with images of last night and his belly full with the fare he had swiped here and there during his social calls.

All in all, he is quite pleased with himself, for his hunger was appeased. That is wisdom itself, he muses.

In the peacefulness of this morning, he thought back to the evenings of his childhood. They were long gone, ten years at least. The sights and sounds had remained with him—the fresh wood, the banana tree's moist leaves, the fields nestled right up to the hills, bulls bellowing their greatness, and cows reflecting the sunset's soft orange light. He recalled the dusk ushering in those childhood nights. Even now, he can see it all.

When the sun departed, evening would sweep in, and the biting cold breezes that crouched in the valley's depths would climb the hills and skim the houses preparing for night. They would catch the smoke rising from chimneys, and then, in passing, greet the youths returning home with water jugs on their heads.

Everyone was heading home, up to the hamlets perched on the hills. Slowly, in fits and starts, in the company of good friends.

He remembered how a hint of cold wind would join forces with the moon to enter the courtyards encircling the Harihais' homes, and slyly set about tickling the peaceful country's children. The little rug rats had no fear of such provocations: they were safeguarded by a short-sleeved shirt or a light sweater, paired with shorts here or a skirt there. The children played with elements of nature, for they were nature. *Umwana si uwumwe*, tradition reminded them: "A child does not belong to any one person exclusively," even its father or mother. That was how the elders explained that all families were linked. All formed but one: the community of life. Life was transferred during birth, it fed on nature and was made real through it. *Umwana si uwumwe*. The child— that bit of humanity, that bud of life—belonged to none except nature. To its fellow creatures and to its cradle, earth. Joyous, it was with trust then that Hariho's chil-

dren threw their small frames into the cold evening.
Trust and courage.

His right foot is folded beneath his buttock. His eyes are
distant. On one side lies a shepherd's crook he has skill-
fully decorated with interlacing black lines. Occasionally,
he nods gently. Those all-nighters can be punishing.

At ten years of age, he began venturing out from the
family seclusion to play in the neighboring households.
He heard new stories. He ate new dishes. He was content
when he returned home late, around eight in the evening.
Sometimes he would have a second meal, prepared this
time by his mother's thin fingers. A strange idiosyncrasy
of hers was that from a very young age she had refused to
wear sandals. She maintained that they were uncomfort-
able, that the soles of her *babouches* distanced her from the
nourishing earth. Her own mother would clean out the
impressive crevices in her feet, black with dust, before
each neighborhood party.

As for his father, in accordance with his age and generation, he wore an *ikoti*, a long black jacket that he alternat-
ed with a baggy gray sweater that reeked of tobacco. His
father spoke little and drank much. Always in silence. He
would take stock of the day, buried in a cloud of pungent
smoke, silver wisps escaping his smooth dark lips. These
fluids swept before his eyes, teary but lively, yellowing
the enamel of his teeth, once white as milk, and climbed
back up the black walls of the house. For a long while
his father would remain crouched before the fire, his son
imitating him. Words were rare in that family, laughter
even rarer.

His memories flow peacefully as the nearby stream.
Other men—elsewhere, not those of this quiet abode—

those men had their fields, cows, goats, and hogs to yield a profit, and bottles to finish off with one another each evening. His father had known those men only a little. In the last few months preceding his parents' "departure," his father had burrowed deeper and deeper into his jacket. Was it fear of the cold perhaps? A sign of fragility, his limbs forgetting how to warm themselves? He would return home early, only to busy himself by stubbornly wandering the fields around his *rugo*. Then, with the sun's departure, he would go in quest of banana beer. Returning home, he would sit back down beside the hearth to sip alcohol that he would never finish.

His father rarely spoke to him. He had never seen him wash his jacket. Eventually the thick material had become an extension of his skin. Nyamuragi had come to believe that his father suffered, but, in the reverie that pervaded their dwelling place, suffering was grounded in silence and so, unencumbered, the world pressed on.

His eyes still riveted to the stream, Nyamuragi lets a sigh escape. Life goes on.

He stretches his neck toward the lapping water of the Tuzi, a stream that skirts the southern edge of Kanya. Nyamuragi has just washed his face, calm and serene. The reflection in the earth's lifeblood mirrors back a light complexion, a full, but rather short beard with very black and very thick hair standing on end, dark eyes, and a nose that is a little too large, a little too pointed, and all too human.

Nyamuragi, the mute, has spent a good quarter hour asking himself where the water comes from. But to this weighty question he has found no response. He is superstitious; he believes in man. And since one should seek meaning only in the comprehensible, he endeavors to come to terms with his fear of man. Man dismantles, creates, and destroys again. That much is apparent.

Behold, the master of this world.

On the bank of the Tuzi, not far from the mute, women—or rather girls—converse. They have come to draw water. It is cold. Some phrases to spice up the morning won't hurt anyone, especially not the birds recounting their dreams in the distance.

"*Mahoro, Kige*" "Peace, girl."

They respond, "And peace to you!"

"Have you found your aunt's chicken?"

"No, unfortunately! And I can't possibly understand where she might have spent the night! Perhaps someone stole her?" It was inconceivable that a chicken could get lost.

"Nyamuragi seems to be lost in his thoughts today!" adds Kigeme.

Hearing his name, he turns his hairy body towards the two conversing adolescents. With a smile. His name often bothers him. He knows what it means, but he doesn't believe that he belongs to the category of mutes. Nyamuragi is well aware that the mouth's sounds come from oscillating jaws and a deft tongue quivering in the palate. Both parts function marvelously for him. His strong teeth are particularly renowned in these parts—they serve as an emergency bottle opener.

He dismantles chicken and other meats with force, gleefully cleaving beef and pork apart with no discrimination whatsoever. His tongue is a trusted weapon in that great battle to which he has been summoned: He loves to eat.

Nyamuragi is often hungry. His round belly sticks out so much that he can barely manage to cover it all up with his ochre sweater. It sticks up just above a black pair of pants, which are rolled up to the ankles and held together by pins and two multi-colored buttons. The ensemble is covered by a jacket, which is also black with orange stripes. Nyamuragi meticulously cares for every inch of his six foot one figure.

He eats much and with gusto, drinking beer as well. He rarely gets drunk, preferring instead to laugh at the spectacle of others who do. It entertains him: their vice is drink. His is gluttony.

On the Tuzi, one of the young girls leaves the area. Her container full of water, she says, "Well, I'm off to look for some sweet potatoes to cook for lunch. And then this afternoon, you know my aunt is expecting guests…"

Kigeme responds, "Ah! *Nshimi*, thank God. Remind your little brother to bring back the top he took. In any case, we'll see each other this evening. I'll be staying a little longer to wash my jumper."

Nyamuragi doesn't understand how it is that he is mute! His jaw works. His tongue works. The main thing is to produce clear and audible sounds, words and phrases that are meaningful.

When he was still very little, four years of age, his mother took him to see a wise relative to diagnose his sickness. The verdict returned: The boy is in good health, he simply doesn't want to speak! There was nothing more to say. It was clear. He wasn't sick, it was all a masquerade. His father had grumbled that evening, before plunging his thin straw into the calabash full of *urwarwa*, banana beer.

Nyamuragi had learned too early, and at his own expense, that life is composed of dualities. Coming and going. Rising up and falling down. Left, then right. Before, after. Crying and laughing. Working and sleeping. Fatigue and rest. Hunger, then a meal. Drinking, then thirst. The tree that grows and the axe that lays it low. The cow's udder swells, and tugging fingers empty it. The snake bites, and a club smashes its head. To give and to receive. Here and there. Above, below. Sow and reap. Youth running all over, old age running to its end. The fat muscle, the bare bone. Living and dying. Cries of joy, laughs of pain. No! Perhaps crying and laughing. Joy and laughter. As long as that duality is present in every breath, life will continue with ease; between the two poles of the duality, everything can be compared. Take the two phases of the cycle: mix them up and you will confuse yourself—pain, joy, crying, laughing. Nothing is certain anymore. Everything is all mixed up—even earth and heaven!

Early on, Nyamuragi had learned the relativity of things and the infinite richness of reality. He was born a connoisseur.

All of a sudden, his stomach's rumbling tears Nyamuragi from his soliloquy. He seeks a way to quiet it. Honestly, he doesn't like when it shouts down there, from his depths… it foretells the troublesome effort of relieving himself. And hunger, of course.

Nyamuragi the mute knows that he has drunk too much water this morning. Its consequences have now arrived in the form of rage and disorder under his jacket.

It is impossible to relieve himself at this stream. It's a public place. But down in his intestines it is boiling. He has to go now! But where? Where to rid himself of this thing? If only he were on the other side of the hill, nearer to his place.

His stomach's rumbling becomes more insistent. His look becomes more imploring. Some place! A small one even! The urgency of his need deforms the features of his face. All of a sudden he rushes towards the young Kigeme, just as she places the ten-liter container on her head to take it home.

Kigeme sees the man bearing down on her. Steadily, silently. Alone.

Suddenly, the young girl recalls the descriptions of the rape of her friend a few weeks ago. Her friend had spoken of a fixed and burning gaze, of the folds in his forehead, the hands that seized her without warning in violence and desire. Her friend had told her to yell if she were ever assaulted.

Kigeme is fourteen years old, a full twelve years younger than Nyamuragi. She drops the container from her head, preparing for a struggle, compulsively pulling her things to herself. Her back is bent; she is scared—a terrified, lost girl. She struggles, while these thoughts rush through her head. She resists the coercive grip that pulls her from the stream to cart her off to who knows where…

"*Ni ibiki?*" What is it? she asks. She sees the mute holding his crotch and hears a lively gurgling…

Then suddenly, from the morning silence that colors this struggle, a scream escapes. A strident, loud, terrified scream, "*Mfasha!*" Help me!

The mute tries to smother her screams with his palm. She must calm down, shut up. He doesn't want anything bad; he simply wants her to show him the latrines.

With her hand balled in a fist and her mouth covered, the young girl assumes that she will soon be suffocated.

Her judgment is clouded by the violence. She knows that she may soon be dead.

From the depth of her lungs she screams, bites the palm that is smothering her, and then screams again.

For two months, the obsessive fear of rape has haunted this country's women. Mothers make their little girls wear panties under their wraps when they go to draw water and under their skirts when they go to school, when before they did not. Girls are required to go everywhere in groups.

In two months, six girls have been raped: two on the hill and four nearby. In two months, the rage of Hariho has simmered against potential rapists. Three men were detained, swiftly taken in as suspects. Eleven days passed before they saw freedom again. Two skipped town to Bujumbura. One stayed, and he is not in hiding. Perhaps he feels protected. The rapes come as no surprise, for there are still those who believe that young flesh cures AIDS…

The girl is still screaming. Nyamuragi has not managed to shut her up despite almost two minutes of vigorous attempts. In order to defend herself the girl is doing everything possible to stay in the Tuzi. She knows that the mute will find it more difficult to rape her in water than on solid ground.

Suddenly, above them, a stone whistles by. Men are running to save Kigeme, who screams all the more forcefully. Nyamuragi instinctively senses that the projectile's target is his back. He abruptly pulls the girl from the stream and heads towards the hilly heights. His gurgling stomach surges again. Nyamuragi knows that he should save himself. He sees a dozen people coming towards him, mouths and eyes bent with rage.

To run, to relieve his intestines, and then to explain himself again! The plan is hastily established.

He abandons the young girl who refused to help him, then runs off ahead of her. Coffee plants scrape against his stomach. Rocks fly by his ears. A large stick is thrown, hitting his side… He stays strong. He runs. He trusts in his shepherd's calves. He isn't scared. He knows how to explain himself as soon as the first task is over. First, he must run to hide, relieve himself, and then afterwards return to his pursuers. To calmly explain himself.

But while running he remembers… he cannot speak! How will he explain himself? As soon as he ends up before them, he will have to be swift and precise in order to contain their fury. But how?

No words, no reprieve. He is guilty! His silence condemns him more than his acts. He was running out of instinct. Now he runs in fear.

Nyamuragi knows for certain that he should not rely on his mute mimicry to clear up the misunderstanding with the crowd. Ah! If only he had known he would experience such misfortune, then he would have learned to speak! His heart is beating quickly. He sees the young girl from the stream again.

The world is a complicated, crazy, and dangerous place, says the mute Nyamuragi to himself as he flees, swearing by all the devils and all the gods in a language that he alone understands.

Uw'ivyago vyagiye n'ivyatsi ntibimubisira
**When tragedy assails you,
even the plants along the footpath impede your way**

Nyamuragi runs quickly. He knows this hill and its slopes. Every evening he walks along them, pleased to survey his own small domain. The land of his fathers. It was many years ago that he was born here. A boy, the son of a man and woman who lived further upstream along this little brook where he washed his face this morning. He sees flashes of his life parade past, details of moments when his parents were still alive, like that evening when he cut his calf with a sickle while trying to throw it at a stubborn lamb.

When he saw blood flowing that evening, he contemplated the sacredness that resides in every animal. He thinks of *intama*, the sheep. White and peaceful. God himself wouldn't know how to dress as white nor be as peaceful. A strange animal that rarely lifts its head. The ram has a husky, fitful voice and a perpetually drooping head. The elders were not wrong; it is an animal to fear.

He had a large family. In his boyhood they were seven: his two parents, himself, three lambs, and a ram. Nyamuragi would take the flock to pasture all by himself, a task he did not relish. He wanted animals that brought him to life with cries of confusion and attempted to escape from his watchful eye! Not these studious miscreants, honest to a fault, calmly looking for grass in the wood, and then plodding back to the *rugo* in perfect obedience. With them everything was so predictable! He would have preferred a rebellious goat—intractable, with a black back that he could lash with a young rod. In the end, the mute did not learn how to be a shepherd. No, he became a thinker.

His parents would go to the fields in the morning, and Nyamuragi would lead his sheep out. Surrounded by those peaceful companions, he reveled in a silence that was playful above all else. Slowly taking the sheep to pasture became a delightful tradition for the little boy. It allowed him to be a man. He learned to observe, to listen, to be patient and, meek as a lamb, to share the warm fur of his beasts when evening visited the family abode. There was a true camaraderie. Occasionally he would even steal corn sheaves to give them. But life with those beasts was painfully predictable!

When he was nine, accompanied only by his sheep, he began to observe men walking their fields. Perpetually at his side, his animals annoyed him because he wanted more sheep. But his parents were not very rich. They didn't have more than the four sheep to give him. Each time he watched his old neighbors passing by from his perch, he thought about Hop-o'-My-Thumb, the small, clever, youngest one who meandered along, tossing out white pebbles the length of his route. They were small beings making their way along paths of ochre earth, on well-trodden bare soil that was dense, naked, and slippery when rain decided to visit. Each one walking by. Miniatures, he observed them from on high. All of which discouraged him from speaking.

Then, when he was 14, his parents died; murdered in a din of harrowing screams! He remembered his mother's terror, her dying curses, the blood that had run, soaking their small home's entryway mats. Red, then black. A sickening odor. His father, who had resisted, had managed but one small blow—a pestle strike—on the neck of one of the killers. The jumbled goodbye shouts… Nyamuragi had hidden himself far away in the depths of his parents' bedroom, and the monsters had not bothered to check the back of that unfortunate house. They had intended, of course, to make off with his sheep. Their lives were worth as much as his parents'—war had reached a fever pitch. All of which made him decidedly unwilling to speak.

While she was alive, his mother had taken him back to consult with the healer, the *mupfumu*, in order to determine once and for all the source of his muteness. The healer was new in the area, a specialist of very high caliber whose opinion was prized. The wise man had determined that it was a serious case: the child brought to him had the *ikirimi*, an unfortunate sickness that blocked the tongue and kept Nyamuragi from speaking. *Ururimi*, the tongue. The healer prescribed surgery for Nyamuragi. Rummaging around in his throat, he cut a few small veins and then administered some bitter leaves to be gargled each morning. The little boy bled. And then he became truly mute. He would have preferred to tell his mother that in the beginning he simply did not want to speak, but the good woman would not have understood. She considered him some sort of victim. Which was knowingly confirmed by the healer. He required a cure, and the prescribed cure had been carefully administered. In the end, it precluded any possibility of ever speaking again.

With the death of his parents whirring in his ears, Nyamuragi withdrew all trust from the words of men. He told himself that nothing remained but to examine their deeds. One night he fell asleep to the noise of his mother's feet, the trembling voice of his father and his paternal breath reeking of alcohol, and the next he fell asleep to the freezing echo of their death and the morbid aroma of their decomposing bodies!

From this state of affairs, he had deduced one thing: Man is all-powerful. He is to be feared. And fear, at its root, is but an unspoken questioning.

He had made a vow to hold his tongue. He enclosed himself in a silence as thick as the wool of his sheep and his big-headed ram. Since then he had despised words. He believed in gestures and things. It wasn't from some long and grandiose pronouncement that his parents had died, but from machetes and hate, from the lethal blow of an axe. Because of this, he had been uprooted. The growing tree, the axe that lays it low… deadly things.

So that is the story of Nyamuragi, the man who was running and jumping, dodging and sweating in Kanya's fresh morning air, all while he pondered how best to demonstrate his innocence.

The huge misfortune, as he understood it, was to show up at the creek, when he never usually went over to that side in the morning. And if he dared to stop, they would capture him, because he is now a freak of nature.

A freak of nature. Little Hop-o'-My-Thumb. His mother… Nyamuragi stops in dismay! He turns towards his pursuers. The mute finally understands: with the hills so completely mobilized, he cannot go on running indefinitely. What's more, since he cannot learn to speak in these few minutes on the run, it is better to just turn himself in. He will try to defend himself with gestures, as he has always done until now.

Suddenly, he is knocked over and seized by the collar. The gnarled stick of an avocado tree breaks against his sweaty back. It hurts. He begins to cry. The pain of mis-understanding. He tries to disentangle himself from the hands clasping his forearms. He flails. He wants to explain himself. But in a squirming that reads like a new attempt to flee, there seems to be only one response. A vigorous hoe handle to the head. Swung by a woman. He has the time to see her raise the handle, the image of his father... But he faints before the blow can even reach him!

Nyamuragi is dragged up the hill. Cries gush forth. The people will carry out the sentence! No court hearing is to be held, but what else is to be done? The deeds are too serious. "Uproot the evil from among your children!" the heart of Kanya thunders.

IV

Uwufise umuringa agira ngo aranuka
The owner of a white necklace doesn't
acknowledge its whiteness

Now let us return to the Tuzi riverbed, the spring of misfortunes. Kigeme lies collapsed on the ground. The young girl is in shock. Shivering, her body no longer belongs to herself. It is nine in the morning, and what was refreshed by the night is now being kneaded with heat by the sun. Kigeme trembles in fear. The aftermath of her encounter with that cursed mute can be seen in her hanging hands—inert one moment, then shot through the next by an inexorable shiver. The young girl's clothing crumples in disarray.

The local women have come to comfort Kigeme. Her mother came running to aid her child. She took little Kigeme in her arms and clasped the girl against her breast for a long, long time. Breathless. Madly biological. Mother. She murmured calming words to Kigeme, even if she herself was beset by the greatest of apprehensions. Kigeme's maternal aunt herded the two entwined women back towards their home.

Kigeme is shocked to the core. Her heart beats very quickly. The young girl has ceased to speak. In her ears, her earlier cry still resonates, distant and yet close at hand; there, on her lips, ready to go back up her throat, burning, following the images that march before her gaze. Right now, she doesn't see anything anymore. She suffers.

The women accompanying the survivor are crying; long rivulets of tears running down these women's cheeks. It is a familiar experience for them all. Numbered among them is Yvonne Barabigize, whose elbow was recently broken by a Primus bottle briskly pitched at her by her husband after an evening of binging. The aforementioned bottle had joyfully accompanied the husband from the music hall to the dwelling, before causing the terrible accident. It was the most natural way that Yvonne's husband could find to wish her good evening. It is true that the old woman—the respectable woman—had dared to ask her spouse to drink sparingly, given the paltry revenue they drew from selling his cassava, dried in the abundant sun of those days.

In the same crowd, there is a woman who measures almost six feet two inches. She was run out of the house by her husband for being too tall. The strict man of the house preferred to bring another, shorter woman (that is to say, more pliable) under his roof. In the meantime, the unfortunate first wife got her share of blows and insults. She had an infinitely more galling fault: She was too old. Thirty-two years old—practically a spinster.

The procession also includes Rosalie Karabaye—twice married to men who died less than a year later, and then almost killed by the family of a third suitor, eager to protect their relation from such a witch. She fled, abandoning everything from her two inheritances and keeping only the essentials: two children from two different fathers. Rosalie had fled for the first time when she was three, some forty years ago, to a refugee camp. Then, some sixteen years ago, she fled again after returning to the country for a few months. At that time, she lost her first husband. Later, during her second reappearance in Burundi after a return from the refugee camps in Tanzania, her second husband was killed in a murky affair surrounding a property dispute. And finally, ten months ago, Rosalie was definitively chased from her birth hill with a threat of violent death if she ever returned again…

Another paternal cousin agreed to give this serial widow (of two husbands, their goods, and their lands) a hut in Hariho. And for the past nine months she has lived a simple life growing beans there.

Upon seeing the young girl who was almost raped, Rosalie is more loquacious than usual; her sobs are more audible than the rest.

The group hikes up the eastern switchbacks of Kanya's hill to arrive at Kigeme's house. They remain quiet, standing on the cleanly swept ground near their rectangular brick house encircled by several banana trees. They are no longer crying; now they groan. Amidst the protracted sounds of rustling loincloths, hiccups, and enraged cries, each woman recounts, in turn, the details of her misfortunate life. Each face is full of sorrow. Kigeme is tucked away in the midst of this vulnerable community.

Her father has left the premises ahead of time, out of prudence… as well as out of integrity, for he self-consciously remembers not entirely blameless remarks that he has made about his wife on occasion. Before he leaves, four of his male neighbors visit to express their solidarity in this misfortune affecting his family. The five men are standing there. The small children have been shooed away from the area, and the older ones have gone to Nyamuragi's execution. The men stare at the twenty-some combinations of headscarves, wraps, and multi-colored wool

sweaters, and tactlessly comment on the gloomy murmur
rising from the feminine sex below.

They grumble to each other with glances. Little by little
they are moved by the dense sadness of the moment. Their
honor must be avenged because their domain has been
desecrated... *Excuse me! Him! That unfortunate freak of nature. He has desecrated their domain and sullied their wealth...*

*God! Now, that woman is gorgeous, Kigeme's mother, over
there, and the wife of Richard Nzitonda, I'm telling you! And
Pierre Guriro's, you see! And Jean-Marie Barekebavuge's, of
course! And Arcel Izobikora's, wow! And... all the others present at this wake today. My, she is gorgeous!* Arcel murmurs
on the sly, ashamed of not having noticed earlier. *Uwufise
umuringa agira ngo uranuka,* The owner of a necklace han-
dles it contemptuously. The owner of a jewel does not realize its true value. It's when we lose it, or run the risk of
losing it, that we realize just how rich we were... A man's
word is at stake! Action must be taken!

Izobikora turns toward his brothers and summons them
to respond to Nyamuragi's affront. Sullying precious
goods acquired with great value over many years (a dowry, a marriage proposal, and long nights to convince the
shy girl)? No! That'll be enough of that! By raping Kigeme,
the cursed mute has defiled all the other women in the region, and the men of Kanya consider themselves all affect-
ed. It is time to crack down.

Igiti ntikigukora mu jisho kabiri, a beam must not scratch
your eye twice. This morning the criminal almost accomplished his mission: "Let us take advantage of this missed
opportunity!" The vigilant people of Hariho are anxious
to underscore the lesson of this morning! One more rape
would be too many! "Let's go, men! We must defend ourselves!" say the five new judges on their way to join the
People's Court on the hill.

Intumva yumva ari uko amaso atukuye
The stubborn only understand once their eyes turn red

In Kirundi, ejo *means both "yesterday" and "tomorrow"!*

This revelation occurs to the old woman on the footpath behind the mute.

*Tomorrow and yesterday: two different times, a single word to label them both. Two places in time, a single name. As a result, one becomes the other. Perhaps this is a linguistic mistake. Or maybe "tomorrow" and "yesterday" meld into one another, because they contain two chimeras: past and future. Perhaps we just haven't been able to find a better word to refer to the content of time gone by than the one for time to come. An oversight? A mistake? A consciousness of the present's pre-eminence? The present…*The one-eyed woman smiles, chewing a blade of grass between her tobacco-stained teeth.

She has just watched the violent arrest of the young mute by his pursuers. She saw the hate that fortified their actions, screwing up their eyes and quaking the knotted veins of their fingers—their rage to punish.

She saw the leader of the pack stirring up his crowd. His fingers frenetically gripping Nyamuragi's motionless wrist, he ordered them to yank the drowsy viper to his feet and then up towards Kanya's heights. In a roar of vengeful anger, he gave the command to prepare a solid, virgin rope. The act of purification they were about to carry out, he explained, required a strong and sturdy hemp rope, previously untouched. They had to punish the vermin, because law is weaker than crime, because it allows a killer to live. The deed comes back on the man. Eliminate the impure man and you protect yourself from evil. Crystal-clear, the message goes down smoothly in this crowd, overheated with anger and thirsty for rain.

The one-eyed old woman watches them drag the mute's body by, gashes taking shape on his skin. Through the bloodied rags of his clothes, she glimpses his round navel whipped by brambles and coated with dust stirred up by the crowd. She realizes they are going to kill him. Now she wishes to mourn the dead.

This unfortunate here-earth. Some would say "here-below." But "below" supposes "above." And for the one-eyed woman, the word "above" (that is, capital A "Above", domain of gods and graces) is unknown to her. Nothing remains for her but the present: forest, waters, trees, ground, men, good, evil… earth. Here-earth. Here, earth—its forests, its places, and its voices. A choice: the present. For these people of Hariho, and even further out, what counts is the present.

The one-eyed woman was careful walking behind the enraged men. She values her kids. She reflects on the mystery of *ejo*.

How, in the language of shepherds, cultivators of the earth and comrades in fur and plants—how, in the language of time's sentinels, could two fundamental concepts of temporal reference be confused: tomorrow and yesterday?

Perhaps these people wanted to consecrate the present by establishing past and future within the same word. To reconsider an ancient notion is a formidable undertaking. Time and man. "What does man live through?" perhaps our ancestors asked themselves.

Through the past? No, because it is but a bundle of memories. At most, things are relived.

Through the future? Alas! Not that either, because it falls under the category of conjecture. At most, we can only dream of it.

Man and time are linked by the present, they must have concluded! A day gone by, a day to come: a single name, ejo. *Certainly, the future had its designation:* kazoza, *literally "what will come." The past as well,* akahise, *"what has happened." But the blunder had been committed. The consequences of which will follow.*

Because Nyamuragi has just awoken from his coma...

Nyamuragi fears the past! He loves the present, which is why he loves to eat. Nature's flavors on his lips, the communion of being: his tongue and dishes. He loves to see a bean, dark or light, become altogether yellow in palm oil, cheerfully sitting next to a piece of sweet potato at the bottom of a dish. He loves the shyness of corncobs, which stay covered up even as their backsides roast. He loves apples too, and cassava with its soft paste that gets on so well with *ndagala*, the fry from Tanganyika.

Above all, Nyamuragi adores rice—white, copious, beloved. To eat is to savor the present! It is to quench hunger, to fully possess the present, to carry life on in peace... The past rekindles memories and creates a pit in the stomach incapable of being filled. Long live the present! And his mouth. In order to forget his tormented past and the horrors that mark his dreams, he eats. He shows up at parties, and he sits there with the others. And eats. In communion.

They have decided to carry him up to the execution site, his improvised bailiff's aggressive handling causes his torso to flop from side to side and his limbs to overextend. Blood spatters here and there. When the ringleader of the vengeful mob sees Nyamuragi's red eye open, a sudden anger seizes him: the crimson glow betrays his monstrosity. An eye is never that red without reason! "*Wa gipfu c'umugabo*" "You degenerate excuse for a man," rages the vigilante judge as he spits in his face.

On Nyamuragi's aching lips, a cry begins to form. In the cursed man's mind, it is "*ego!*" or "yes" that he pronounces. Terrorized, in anticipation of death, he humbly acquiesces. He takes upon himself the responsibility for all of humanity's faults... "Yes!" The impotent judgment of the crushed! The Court hears something else, however. "*Ejo!*" escapes his mouth, his lips producing the word for "tomorrow" or maybe even "yesterday"... These ad hoc jurors, however, only have so much time to deliberate. *Ejo?*

The other man, the makeshift head of the People's Court of Kanya, understands "yesterday" and lets Nyamuragi go! He calls the breathless crowd that has gathered around the soon-to-be-hanged body to witness, repeating "*ejo! ejo!...*" In a burst of clarity, Nyamuragi attempts to seize this moment of respite. He gives the only defense possible, a cry of "*ejo!*" which is, once again, nothing more than a mispronunciation of "*ego!*"

Foaming at the mouth, the mute has accepted his lot. He has ceased to offer up any resistance: Yes, he is everything, even evil incarnate. Let his suffering be shortened. Let him be pardoned or destroyed as quickly as possible. "*Ego!* I am a killer!" the mute seems to mean, *ego!* maybe to amuse the crowd… The police will intervene shortly. He hears a murmur from the other side of the crowd. It is an *ego!* of compassion for him! Then the crowd begins to bicker.

An uproar of murmurs and yells! The defendant's word has managed to move the jurors. As quickly as possible they must rule on this new piece of evidence that has just been added to an already overwhelming list.

Let us see, the jury says to itself, *So yesterday,* ejo, *there was in fact some shouting about a robbery in a household about four hills from here… Is Nyamuragi admitting to another crime and adding to his disconcerting total? Or tomorrow,* ejo, *the day of Passover…*

May the suffering of the Divine Child remind you of the insignificance of this runt we're about to torture. May we grant him grace. In the holy season we simply do not hang. Adjourn this business out of respect for your faith… agrees the other half of the interpreters of Nyamuragi's *ejo*.

In short, it is possible to discern sounds coming from the mute who speaks! Let's get a hold of ourselves so we can better deal with this matter with all the diligence and solemnity required by a work of public hygiene. Let's shut him up! the jurors and executioners of the People's Court say to themselves. A club smashes the troublemaker's skull, silencing him. A second fainting. *Blood runs, o people of Kanya.*

In fury, the leader of the masses commands the motionless body again, "*Ntiwiryamishe sha, urakabona uno munsi!*" "Don't pretend you've fallen asleep. You're about to get it now!"

VI

Umuryambwa aba umwe agatukisha umuryango
**Even if the evil-doer acts alone,
the fault falls on his entire family.**

The cry comes swiftly in this savage trial. *"Wa gipfu we"* "you soulless creature, you waste of space," shrieks a young girl, her face chastened with restrained fury. The accused newcomer rises up. Two gazes meet: instant mutual loathing!

"Wa mukobwa we, untukiye iki?" "You girl, why do you insult me?"

She replies furiously with sounds of scorn: *"Fyofyofy-ofyo...."*

Outraged, she continues: *"Aho ubona war'uriko ugiriki?"* "What did you think you were doing?" The enraged face of the Harihai girl is defiant. Her hands fly here and there. And her right foot thumps the ground, scattering thick dust. A misunderstanding? Cowardice? Let's leave the flying insults to review the deed that provoked this new altercation.

The girl who was insulted is Irakoze, a name that means "thank you God." In a reverent gesture, her parents indicated their gratitude to the Creator for their child's health. She grew up in Hariho, but left the noble country for Gitega in order to continue her studies. She is 20 years old, with rather capable lungs (something the public is about to discover), only two years short of finishing her studies. Well, add another year of unforeseen events… so, in three years Irakoze reckons she will be ready to dedicate herself to a husband. Her womanly figure is stirring: Irakoze is a gorgeous girl. The tragedy is that she has come to the bar of this People's Court accompanied by a young man who is a connoisseur of works of art like her. The clash is jarring!

His name is Corneille Mugabo, which means "man," and he is a former cook from Bujumbura, recently employed as a bus driver. In his stormy youth he was known for flouting the law. Currently, he is married.

Like other members of this vigilante jury, just a while ago, Irakoze was unreservedly launching cries of anathema against the criminal dozing there in the center of the crowd. Carried away by the moment, her faded blue t-shirt lifted slightly… and the firm flesh of her hip was exposed.

Mugabo, the connoisseur of art, simply could not repress the urge to slide his hand onto the exposed flesh! Like the chisel of a sculptor… it was a lost gesture from his turbulent youth in Bujumbura—that furnace of lust and Homeric drinking sessions—or perhaps it was a gesture that reminded him of married life here in Kanya. In truth, it was not an act of joy, at least not compared with what he lived every Monday in the Bwiza "5 on 5" nightclub.

To live is to link each moment with the next. It is to ensure that a former cook remains the same today as he reels in clients for a bus journey to the country's interior. It is to function such that the lust for life that once guided the hedonist in Bujumbura remains unchanged now that he plays the family man in Hariho.

That is living—even at the risk of betraying himself or of feeding off his past to fully enjoy the present. And Corneille the connoisseur knows this. Has he not learned that art's function is to pause the motion of life? It is meant to freeze the scene, grasp a moment of time in mid-air as it spreads its wings to vanish after coming to fulfillment, catch hold of a single gesture flowing in the river of action, create a sound that captures one emotion from the infinite combinations of tone, and pitch to create a solitary buoy bobbing back and forth in the immense hubbub of daily life. Art unfastens a moment from time by freezing the scene. And yet it is not hostile to life. Therein lies its worth… A piece of art establishes a point of reference. It cuts a scene from the overflowing march of events in order to enlarge it, thicken it, enrich it, strip it bare, and then share it with others.

That is what the sight of Irakoze's round navel has done—it has stopped everything around him and created a gravitational bubble between that small abdominal hollow and Corneille's astute gaze.

Life is a series of meals that we must learn to savor in the face of expired condiments and second-hand ingredients. Sometimes we appreciate them. Often we do not. Above all, it is about not starving to death. So we eat, and we endeavor to take pleasure from it. And then after eating comes a moment of calm… A moment of reflection, when we know that death has not taken us away just yet, at least not in this precise moment of rest after eating, this connoisseur moment. In this instant, it is not fundamentally about wanting to thicken the sauce with cassava paste or adding a few rice balls to a handful of beans floating in a tender sea of palm oil. In this instant, it is about living… in this very instant! With bellies bulging, we reflect on our satisfaction. Nothing else. For that matter, we are so content that we cannot wait to doze off. A connoisseur moment, which becomes complete by the *ukwinovora*, the licking of one's lips.

In general, this gesture occurs just after we have finished eating, around the time of the burp. In that precise moment, mislaid traces of recently consumed dishes show around the aforementioned lips. The tongue comes through to gather the crumbs and polish the teeth and lips. Preparing the oral apparatus for another struggle, the tongue's movement is instinctive, nonchalant, much like the movement of the artist's hand.

It is understandable: the *ukwinovora* comes after the meal. Dreamer that he is, Mugabo placed this action of the eminent connoisseur before the meal, a meal, he laments, that was far from guaranteed…

Irakoze, whose skin has just been defiled, cackles: "*Ahubwo nawe n'ukukugira nk'uwurihano.*" "Actually, Mugabo, you also deserve the punishment reserved for this unfortunate mute!" The crowd, momentarily surprised by the intensity of the oral sparring, turns towards Mugabo. The wait for his reply takes a long time. Too long, a whole second. Then the man finally responds: "*Mwa bakobwa bo mu gisagara nta ndero mukigira.*" "It's you city girls! You deserve it, you who have lost your good manners…"

The brawl resumes with greater intensity! Some (the most numerous here) have understood that this girl is an example of the urban youth's moral decadence. Curses fly: May disgrace be upon this endangered species! Because as Mugabo "the man" tells it—and what a shame for this country—Irakoze has dared to let her navel out into the open air, and in public, I'll have you know, during the proceedings of a trial! Ah! Such a crime, such a taboo! They loudly and energetically lament the decadent youth these days, lacking in moral fiber, the eternal *abana b'ubu nta kintu*, today's children aren't worth anything any more.

Others have interpreted Mugabo's slow response as an admission of weakness. It is well known that, in public insults, one should never let the other speak alone. One must expand vocally, occupying the entirety of the space reserved for both to speak. In general the vanquished one is the one who dares allow his tongue to rest. One must speak a great deal, insult, wonder aloud, monologue even more loudly, mock, challenge, deplore, become outraged often, throw out a proverb, evade the questions of one's partner above all… In this People's Court bewildered for the second time, the most numerous were of the first opinion.

The most aggressive, the small remainder that hasn't lashed out at Mugabo, are composed of young people. Meanwhile, acid remarks fly from Mugabo's head to Irakoze's, then return, setting off again, little by little—and it's understandable, youth is capable of so much—before finally focusing on Mugabo. At the sight of the beautiful girl who gesticulates in outrage, the sympathy spontaneously spreads out to a fringe of the assembly. Such a woman would not know how to lie. All the more so as, just a little bit ago—important reminder—the one accused of impropriety was not spontaneous in his reaction. There is an eel under a boulder—or, excuse me, a mole under a hill. Down with the impolite one!

Mugabo senses that the wind has changed—for him things have gone from bad to worse! Even his first defenders have changed sides. Slowly, faces harden to his replies…

The married men speak little, and that is saying a lot. One of their own has been caught red-handed in infidelity. The wives holding court here lash out at the guilty glutton. The unfortunate Mugabo sees twenty, thirty… fifty mouths cursing at him, spitting on his humble person… No more time for pretense, the beast has been hunted and will soon be captured; Mugabo sweats from shame and beats a retreat.

What he has not understood is that a voracious fringe surrounds him and Nyamuragi, composed of the women whose daughters could at any instant be identically sullied, the wives who risk such an affront, and the adolescent girls enraged by such barbaric treatment. Sides have been taken. Corneille flees.

What he had not gathered in the whirlwind of outraged women and angry cries is that something is happening in Hariho: the country is being purified of abominable vices like rape and infidelity.

Now that Mugabo has just escaped the public rage, the claws of the People's Court turn once again towards the sleeping man who has dared to wake up again. Two large bumps crown his dusty-haired head, clotted blood is glued to his temples, and two front teeth are missing.

The crowd continues to reverberate: The wrong that Nyamuragi has done must be cleansed! The chief ranter thunders the masculine oath: *"Ndakambura umukobwanje!"* "May I undress my girl!" Faced with these two renegades who have just despicably sullied the masculine race in the presence of all, the men holding court here have understood that an act of piety is necessary now: to renew their marriage vows and, in blood, to utter once again the words "I love you", showing they are fully alive to their dearly beloved spouses, quivering with rage in the fray. They must reassure their daughters that nothing will sully them as long as the memory of this country lives on.

The feminine barrier encircling the wounded body of Nyamuragi is broken, pushed apart by the strength of fathers, young fiancés, and other adolescents eager to throw themselves into the task of recovering their honor! The head of the pack divides up the tasks, pushing away the women who are the least surly. The unfortunate gash sprawling on the earth no longer has the strength even to speak. They take him from both sides, a foot for one, an arm for another, a female fist in the armpit, yanked in four directions and dragged up towards the heights of Golgotha.

VII

Bukebuke bushikana umusiba ku mugezi
Only with great patience does the worm reach the stream

The one-eyed woman follows the crowd. Trailing behind her like bad company, her goats and memories are poor companions. She was just saying to herself, "It is a strange way to make an oath upon the forbidden—*Ndakambura umukobwanje!*" In our times, some go even further: *Ndakenda imbwa!*" "May I fuck a dog!" A far cry from decency, but it is one of those things that people say.

The old woman is still turning these things over in her head. Wordlessly, far from the chaos before her eye, far from these powerful, hasty young men, far from the violent anger of the impotent. She reflects in wonder on how the forbidden has moved from curse to deed in such little time, an illicit transferal. Pensively, she remembers her own father, a blunt, thin man, who was very strong and who loved to return home a little drunk some evenings. His curses were all related to her, the only daughter of a rich, forty-cow farmer. What would he say today if he were still alive? If he came home some jet-black night back then and tripped on one of the large trunks that sealed off the family lot? Would that same curse even make sense today?

The one-eyed woman thinks that the curse is taking its revenge for decades of overuse. *From repeated invocation, the shameful now takes place! In these days we actually uncover our daughters!* She heard it on the radio... *We rape others' daughters, the knees of Burundian women are disgracefully exposed...* She stops herself, too embarrassed to even think of such monstrosities. The old woman chews on a long blade of grass that tastes raw and sandy. The discomfort makes her nervous.

She remembers that paradoxically, far away in those cities that she has traipsed through two or three times in these last two years, men don't swear by the ordinary any more. That is to say, they cannot be trusted. Their word no longer has the sacred as anchor. The curse has become an affront and an insult to good moral standards. If a man said, "*Ndakambura umukobwanje sinivye ayo mahera!*" "May I undress my daughter if I stole that money!" it would no longer provoke strong confidence. Worse: it would likely encourage distrust.

Formerly, it was unimaginable for a father to undress his daughter! Impossible! And that impossibility, ingrained in the heart of the custom, made that reality impossible to conceive. Just as the act of sleeping with his daughter was impossible, so stealing that money would have been foreign to him. The horror that the curse evoked drove the audience to believe that the one swearing was not capable of committing the act of which he was accused. It was the era of trust, when people put faith in exchanged words.

Is this the consequence of all these wars? The lie of division has come to roost. Squabbles, suspicions, and doubts were exacerbated by a history of massacres and broken lives. Distrust now lives among the *beneburundi*, those to whom Burundi belongs. So for years now, one's word was readily questioned; it could not be accepted at face value.

Too many deaths have taken away the people's beautiful, united soul. And that unified people had a yardstick: its rich language and speech, *ijambo*.

Ijambo carries a portion of the other. It is an invitation to discovery. *Ijambo*—word, discourse, secret, courteous response. *Ijambo*: speech. *With all this death among us*, the one-eyed woman thinks, *speech has become divided, multiplied, and fragmented. Its unity has been irreparably shattered. So we no longer believe in the curse or the consequences it invokes.*

Speech is no longer carved in stone; it has become a simple veneer, readily abused when a little gust of wind comes, but scarcely worth more. When the confrontation becomes serious, they need evidence! Faith of another world! In public, swearing by "*Ndaka...*" "May I...", now provokes disapproval. If shared, it then becomes disgust.

Since disgust thrives on these images of the forbidden, what happens next is truly nauseating. A poor Harihai who tries to clear his name by swearing in such a way, wanting to prove that he has not stolen the money, will quickly find himself presumed guilty of the act. Out of caution. While waiting for the evidence.

To no longer swear on anything, but to stick to facts. A strange land. This dry wind, these silent woods, these blue skies, this sterile and impure soil! A strange land. With a deft blow of her crook, she reprimands one of her goats feasting on weeds. And she sighs. The beast sighs as well: what a harsh mistress!

VIII

Bibwirwa benshi bikumva benevyo
**What is said to many is only
understood by those concerned**

"Give me that squash over there, the cracked one!"

"Get a move on it, your shoulders bother me! And what are you doing in my store in the first place, you ridiculous excuse for a black-eyed man? So, you're not going to get anything?"

"Two! Two tomatoes for a hundred francs! I only sell things in Burundian francs. I am a simple man. Dollars I'll willingly take, but I know that you are poor!"

"You idiot with your ears plugged shut! Sweet Jesus, what did you say?"

"There! Look at the ass on that woman! You might even say it was my tender Shishiro, the well endowed. May God preserve her!"

"One rope, and make it a good one!"

"The colors of this sock remind me of a slug. With its shiny, disgusting, glistening threads! They're even elastic. Soooocks!"

"It's hot out, yet people don't want to drink my tea! I'm going to have to change the menu up and offer them cold tea! You over there, do you know how to make cold tea? Yes, you, selling cold stuff! Hey!"

"My father told me this morning that they've caught a big-time crook. He ran for almost six hills before the people caught up to him, and then they still had to sic the dogs on him. A guy who stinks like swine, with gigantic toes and hands like old banana tree leaves. He speaks strangely."

"It's been a long time since I heard tell of you! You work in Bujumbura now? My little girl is about to turn three now, and I think that I should knock up my wife and see if I can get a boy. You didn't know the one born after my little girl died? Ooooh yes! You really have become a city boy—no word from your family. Wait a sec! You see that guy with a black goat next to him? No! The bearded one! Yes, yes! That's the one! They only just found out that he's actually a sorcerer! He's as dark as his goat!"

"Hey man, why you looking at my sweaters? You want to buy something?"

"So, shall we go? I brought a condom! Quick, before my wife comes back from the market! Are you scared? But of what? Me? Well are you sick, or what? Anyway, you're not going to heaven with that thing of yours, better enjoy life here on earth! Ready to go?"

"Noooooooooo! I already told you: one kilo of Sosumo sugar!"

"O Lord, how will I get two hundred francs? It's not much, but I still need two hundred for these pills? It's theft, that's what it is! When they cost three hundred in the health center! It's almost the same price, there's no difference! People these days are so dishonest, may I die a quick death!"

"I said a rope! Peace, my brother! I see that you've put all the ropes out here on display, but I want one that has never touched a goat's neck, a dog's back, or a chicken's dry leg. One that has never been wrapped around two tins of banana wine or even been used to tie up a cow with a heavily handled udder. A virgin rope? Yes, I want a totally virgin rope! Right away! It's urgent, I have some business to settle!"

"Your wife isn't cheating on you any more? But I've told you a million times: Women are all liars, every last one of them. They want our money, that's all. Right, it's because they can wait till the cows come home! Hey, your right finger is swollen!"

"This pile of fry costs a thousand francs. I can't do anything about it. Tanganyika is sterile, now nothing grows there anymore… I told you the *ndagala* feed on water and sand. And since the water is dirty and the sand too, we can't get any more fry. They're all dying of hunger! What did you say?… Yes, of course they're more abundant!"

"A rope! White, well-knit, and tested by expert hands! And entirely unused!"

"I've seen it all now! We got national television even here. Kajekurya's son brought one in from Bujumbura, and yesterday we watched the war between the Jews and the Arabs. They're never going to let it go! You know, I learned that even white men are human like us. We saw them sleeping under poorly-pitched tents after a strong wind destroyed their homes. No! I'm like an uncle to him; he can't make me pay up. Instead, I think he's going to open a new cinema to make some money."

"You child, what are you doing here in this market?… Your mother sent you to buy some salt? Here, I'll give you some and you tell her I know she's good for it. Then I'll come by this evening to talk with her about it and make sure you've passed on my message. I see you're wearing slippers!"

"Ooooh! Yalalalala yaaaaaaalalallalla!"

"Get out of my sight!"

"Look at these plump arms of mine! And this shapely rear end! Take a look at how round my shoulders are!"

"A nice fat pig, indeed. Is it for the taking?"

"We caught the troublemaker, flushed out the crook. We're going to punish him right away. Tell your friends here and elsewhere and your families back at home: the people have decided! A rope! A solid rope! Make a gift of this purifying gift to the people!"

"May I knock up my own daughter if you—you—are going to heaven! You? How could you? You've already stolen two goats, copulated with your cousin, and eaten a crow! You're not going to be hanging out with angels in heaven with that kind of blackness on your soul."

"Mommy! Mommy! Can I get this?"

"Two tomatoes for a hundred francs! You take them. Mix them with oil and fry. You'll love it!"

"The dust! It's dust!"

"But you have to add cassava powder. Cassava dough! Hot. Here it's sold for a little more: three cents the bowl!"

"Yeaaaaaaaah!"

"Very early this morning I saw an owl staring at me from the roof of Paul's place. You see, with this market, you have to get up early. And as I was turning right, just behind the big mound of clay, I saw it! The owl was black, its eyes full of ill omen!"

"You whore!"

"He's his only remaining son. His wife died when his eldest son was seven years old and the youngest was five months. Two sons, three sisters. He learned how to cook, his sisters too. Wasn't that rich, the poor man. Had enough to eke out a living, the mornings he would beg for work in the field, and the afternoons he got himself a job as a meat waiter in Ntirumveko's outdoor bar and grill. This way he made himself some money on the side, a little at first, and then the little amount started to grow. Slowly though because he had to send his eldest son to school. He began primary school when he was nine years old. At twenty-five he went to college. At thirty, he died. All the same, old Nibara's second girl has just bought herself a beautiful house, with walls painted all in blue."

"Hello? Hello? Can you hear me? Yes? Tell Claver he should think about sending the ten thousand francs down for his wife's medical costs. She came down with a terrible case of malaria. And then remind Pascaline that she still owes me my two… Hello? Hello?!! Yes… Pascaline, she promised me two bottles of very warm beer. If I don't get them in time, I'll melt in this heat!"

"But it smells good!"

"What? The rope? Yes, I'll take it."

IX

Akatareste kaba gasema
**Cursed is the one who
does not heed warning**

To his unsteady eyes, the sky is red. The clean sky morning has transformed into a bloody glow, pushing through the cracks of his swollen eyelids with spite and fury. His mouth is no more than a ball of muddy flesh mixed with drool and sweat. The torture of this victim (or perhaps we should say this cursed soul) has gone on for too long. Thirty minutes. Thirty minutes: a succession of blows— mostly accurate and excruciatingly painful—unfortunately aimed kicks, and carefully chosen curses. All accompanied by gobs of spit in varying sizes, depending on the saliva stock possessed by each contributor. There is something exceptional about this People's Court. Each member acts as bailiff, supporting witness, defense lawyer, and judge, which complicates the sensible use and normal targeting of their precious glandular liquid.

The defendant, Nyamuragi, has gone from lack of understanding and extreme physical suffering to something much simpler: waiting. His spirit has suffered so much here that he would rather yield all of the space around him to his torturers and take refuge where they surely cannot reach him—within. Like a snail. To curl up within himself. Waiting for the end. That is all he can do to stay alive.

Nyamuragi had never been beaten like this before, not by his parents (may God keep them in His holy palms!) nor by anyone else. You cannot strike a mute: It's like drowning a blind man in light. The action would be an insult to the divine hand that fashioned him. Instead, you knowingly murmur. You accompany him in his world populated with words made of gestures. In the case of the handicapped, it's about meeting him where he is with his condition, showing him that he is still profoundly and essentially human, despite his different physical constitution. It is a sign of respect to lower yourself, to bow down in a gesture of recognition. Recognition of his unfortunate fate but also of your infinite good fortune to have been born whole… It's a gesture that his parents always modeled when Nyamuragi cried about not being able to go to school.

His father explained to him that the white man's way of transmitting knowledge did not respect the handicapped. That did not stop him from sending his only son to the Bazungu school at an early age. But it was a different era. In those times, it was said that a great future was promised to those who managed to study.

The conclusion of that regrettable incident at school, as we are about to discover shortly, was well known in the home of those seven beings. His father muttered its epilogue through the cloud of smoke that permeated the family hut: "The White Man's School is disrespectful of human life. It should welcome all who desire to study and educate them according to their abilities! Why does it choose which ones will come to fruition? Why does it not dedicate itself to all the seeds presented to it by the people? Why does the White Man's School select those who are normal, and not you, my child? The strong, the intelligent, those who know how to speak…"

Nyamuragi cried silently. Then his mother gave him a sweet potato grilled on their home's smoky hearth. The tuber soothed the child's adult anxieties, and the evening went on.

In fact, at a very young age Nyamuragi had loved to read, this way of summarizing life with signs. Letters which possessed hats, ties, crooked dashes, feet, arms pointed upwards or turned downwards, hooks above and below, commas, periods, scrawls and scribbles, with the odd one crossed out. His first month of school he had spent in peace, happy to learn and happy to be forgotten among the other little schoolchildren. He was eight years old. He immediately became attached to his schoolmaster Jean-Paul. But thirty days after the first day of class, his teacher died of old age. The second morning after his teacher's unfortunate demise, a new one arrived. His name was Térence, and that very day he sent Nyamuragi to the board with an assignment to read a new letter they had just learned: d, da, de, di, do, du… those senseless sounds they had to say.

The poor boy couldn't speak. They had forgotten to warn the civil servant in the first grade class at Hariho's primary school about Nyamuragi's situation. At the very least the teacher should have asked the student's name. Instead, Térence, who was completing his second year of service, had plunged the young colts into their lessons the moment he entered the classroom. Without realizing that the chubby little boy was mute. Or else he had known and wanted to yank Nyarweza and Bakundane's son out of his mutism come what may.

The fact remains that the very young mute found himself at the blackboard, whimpering (above all, one must not disobey the schoolmaster's order!) and in despair he diligently began writing: "d, d-a, d-i, d-u, d-o, d-e."

Everyone in the small class began to laugh. A cheerful laugh, as every child is capable of... But the master, moved by who-knows-what bad spirit, maliciously pulled at Nyamuragi's left ear. For a long time the little boy wiped away the tears that were copiously running over his pudgy cheeks. Then he took his slate, the *ikigura*, and slowly left the class, never to return.

Nyamuragi instinctively hated pain. That's why he loved to eat. As his parents only heard the teacher's version—even if they did avoid seeking anything beyond it—and as their only child could not, and above all *did not want*, to speak of that morning when he left school forever, they kept him at home. Especially since, for some time now, his brothers—the sheep—had been feeling a little lonely...

His parents had told him that school is a place that fashions the human spirit, but if that was the case, it was a place where the essential characteristic of that fashioning has been forgotten—respect. *The master could have stopped the other students' jeering. He could have asked me why I didn't want to read his letters. He could have learned to listen to my silence... he didn't need to hurt me!* So, Nyamuragi rehashed the event to himself from the hill heights where he kept company with his sheep. Each evening he learned to mimic the lines awkwardly drawn on his *kigura* by his father... which is why, at eleven years of age, the young Nyamuragi knew how to read and write. Just for himself.

Now, in this forest, his solitude is just as great, despite the enraged cries that continue to climb from the surrounding shadows. Nyamuragi doesn't go to the trouble of listening to them. He can't see any more. He keeps vigil. For himself alone. He patiently awaits death. To die from the consequences of having eaten too much last night. What terrible luck. He has to come to terms with the truth: Life inevitably comes to an end. Strangely.

One night, Nyamuragi had a dream. He was on the bank of a very large pool. The water resembled a giant mirror extending from the sky over the earth. It wasn't completely light, nor totally dark. It was the mysterious atmosphere of a dream in the depths of a troubled night. The water seemed frozen. The air nonexistent.

Then there was a great rock glistening with viscous matter. And onto this rock alighted a colossal lizard with cracked skin and a pair of giant dragonfly wings. The hideous animal's muzzle was pointed towards the sparkling surface of the pond. The eyes, half-hidden behind long, tired eyelids, were completely still. Which gave the impression that the beast was dozing, but at the same time the thing's incredible ugliness was extremely anxiety inducing. Which truly petrified the adolescent. It wasn't the vision of that strange being… but the impression that such a horror could awake, that in spring he, Nyamuragi, might run into it… that glistening beast of life…

Nyamuragi was only twelve at the time of that terrifying dream. For ten minutes or so he had howled, frozen to the ground by that nauseating vision on the mat that served as his bed,. Copious tears escaped his eyes, hands scratching the mat, legs circling in a never-ending flight from the monster watching over that pond. Then his mother came and shook him gently, and the adolescent abruptly tore himself from the awful vision.

He had run to the hearth and then returned to his mother to ask for something to eat. After a few well-weighed mouthfuls, he had gone back to sleep. All in a state of virtual lethargy, brought on by rivulets of tears rolling forth from his misty eyes. Being mute, the next morning he had not been able to explain the reason for this worst of nights to the six members of his family.

Nyamuragi had a principle: never waste time explaining to others what is difficult for him to understand himself. A practice consciously cultivated. Since his expulsion from primary school, he had scarcely tried to make himself understood. He could communicate with gestures. Actions such as convincing, seducing, and discussing, however, were unknown to him. Since then he conceived of them as futile obligations to a community that had confined him to a sub-human category since birth.

Born incomplete, he had settled for living out his inadequacy. Just for himself. Without making it a tragedy or a question of resisting an accursed fate. One must not fear what is. His mother would tell him: *"Ibuye riserutse ntirimena isuka,"* "The pebble that peeks out of the dirt cannot split the hoe." As soon as a farmer sees a pebble starting to show in the ground, he stops and probes at it with his hoe, goes to the trouble of picking it up, throws it a long way off, and then calmly settles back once more into his labor.

What is already is; you must disregard it and continue your life in peace.

A lesson learned from his sheep. Peacefully seeking grass to ravage, attacking it with molar bites and well studied turns of the neck, to calmly chomp, to smell, to swallow their daily portion and then to rest. To ruminate, to diligently re-chomp the grass, without ever searching to explain to your shepherd by any means possible why you are ruminating or why it is only grass you seek. To live your small life, just for yourself. Possibly to wait for killers to come and shorten your owner's life, missing the shepherd and taking you away. Death can occur after all that. It's the natural order of things. Because the essential thing has been done: you have lived your life. In any case, you are born mute for life. And whatever you do, you will have a mute life.

Nyamuragi was born alone. He had never had a conversation. Nor a discussion. Nor a debate. He had been born mute; speech was etched into him. He drew nourishment from it as a matter of course. Awkwardly. Alone. In isolation. He knew no friend, and he had no family to count on. Already when he was still very young, his two parents were cursed at and called witches for wanting to remain isolated in their poverty… In any case, the war had carried them away. Peace be upon their souls!

All these people shouting around him believe they are rendering justice! Justice in this case requires taking the rapist, who was caught in the act, and enclosing him in a cell and an atmosphere of anger, suffering, and terror. So firmly binding him to his crime that if the People's Court devoured the criminal (something that was about to be done, if it didn't displease the sun searing an already overheated space). Then the people would swallow the black millstone that bears upon it all the serious wounds this unfortunate mute has inflicted upon the community of Hariho. This is the most prudent of actions.

No, those who believe the people of Hariho to be naïve are seriously mistaken! They are well-informed; they know the shortest path between two points is a straight line. Between a crime and its redemption, the surest means of arriving safe and sound with a minimum cost is a clearly delivered sentence. In this case, that straight line will be traced by the rope from which the criminal soon will swing.

They have forgotten that *"akatereste kaba gasema"*… "what is, in any case, is"… one shouldn't seek meaning except in the intelligible. They have forgotten that Nyamuragi has always survived alone. Obviously!

Umugani ugana akariho
The proverb molds what exists

For men like *him,* who have served in the army, an order and its execution are one.

Once upon a time, there was an old man who had a very beautiful daughter. A daughter so beautiful that fig leaves bowed whenever she passed by. His daughter drew clean water, brought back dry wood, prepared good meals, meticulously cleaned the house, brewed a most excellent sorghum wine. And she was radiant.

They nicknamed her Inabwiza, she who has beauty. Inabwiza had the fine neck of a heron, the grace of a heifer when she walked, and a harmonious voice when she spoke. She kept her modest eyes low and never burst into laughter.

Her father was unfortunate to have lost his loving wife, but he delighted to see that she did not leave him alone. Inabwiza had nine older brothers, all married, who loved him surpassingly. She was the only girl in that very rich family.

Her brothers had done everything to find her an honorable suitor, with the rank and stature worthy of Inabwiza's beauty and renown. Several fathers came in the name of their sons to ask for her hand. In vain, for the virgin's father had a frightful severity when it came to his daughter's dowry. Any reason was sufficient to delay the departure of his beloved Inabwiza until the last possible moment. Either there were not enough cows or the suitor did not have the right appearance to receive his loving daughter (*umuntu atanga ico afise*, we give only that which we have) or the site of his house was improper, certain to cause unbearable fatigue to his Inabwiza whenever she went to draw water or cut wood, or, quite simply, the man was too poor to even take care of his daughter's moles, let alone her exquisite voice. That required milk, honey, thoughtfulness, and great attention.

The old man was respected by all and detested by a certain number because he had dashed the hopes of those rather attractive young men. He had dared to declare to several fathers that they were too poor! Or to young men that they were a little too vulgar in their speech to be spouses worthy of Inabwiza's virtues...

In the country where he lived, he had become the bane of an entire generation. When he went to sit among the hill's other public figures, they would respectfully make more space than necessary for him, in the crazy hope of wresting his daughter away from him. In the evenings, before he had even begun to drink, he was overwhelmed with invitations for banana wine. To the degree they desired his daughter they courted the old man. All a waste of time.

Time went by, and her brothers kept close watch over Inabwiza unbeknownst to her. Her beauty grew with time, and suitors came from further and further away!

One evening, a young man arrived. He was a stranger, a handsome passerby. Slender as a prince, he spoke with great self-confidence.

"You who reside in these parts, could you assist us in our time of need? We are strangers in this land, and we seek a place to sleep for the night."

The old man was not present that evening, but Inabwiza agreed to welcome him into the *rugo*. Eyes lowered, she served him something to drink. The young man remarked that she had beautiful fingers. Inabwiza smiled and then left the room. She was touched. It was the only moment in which their gazes met that evening.

When the old man returned that evening, he found the stranger seated in silence before the *rugo*'s fire, a lost look upon his face. Only the cows sneezed from time to time.

"Behold a kinsman that my age no longer allows me to recognize!" Inabwiza's father exclaimed. "Who are you from?" he then asked.

"Alas! I am simply passing by, blinded by the thickness of the night, I have begged your dwelling as a lowly place to lie my head and a chance to rest my feet. I come from the north, from a man named Mashomeza. He is my father."

"Ah! We cannot refuse a bed to a passerby, my child! Enter so that you may rest!"

Inabwiza, who always went to bed after her father, brought water to the two men. They washed their hands and ate some peas and squash. At the orders of the master of the household, the stranger received more water to wipe away the dust of the day. He had remained just as he was at his introduction in front of the enclosure.

"You speak well, my son! Could your father be a prince?"

"Oh no! I merely come from a land where everything grows and where men become rich and beautiful thanks to the blessing of the only God."

"And how old are you?" the old man began again.

"Since I was born, my father has counted twenty-one *miganuro* each year's sowing, which is enough to distinguish the sun's glow from the moon's."

Inabwiza's father looked at him for a long time, then smiled. *Behold my son-in-law!* he thought. Unfortunately he was exhausted, as he had spent the entire day inspecting his vast and bountiful fields. He requested that everything possible be done so that his guest would sleep well that night. Outside, the cows sneezed all the more. Inabwiza had noted an unusual commotion in the stable. But she had not said anything about it. She had checked several times, asking the shepherds who slept with the beasts if there might be a thief who had come to hide among her father's many cows.

"*Natwe ntituzi igituma, mwiza.*" "We also do know not why, o beautiful one!" they responded to her.

The night was calm, very calm. Except for the cows... Inabwiza thought that she also heard the stranger go outside. *Nature's calling,* she told herself.

In truth, she barely slept. She thought about the man's appearance, with his 21 years and his strong torso, his way of walking, furtive like a hunter, his strong and certain voice. She imagined again the little purse made of snake or lizard's skin that hung from his neck, his shoulders when he bent over to wash his feet... That night she stayed up very late.

The stranger arose very early the next morning. When the entire household hurried out to milk the cows and sweep the courtyard, they found him seated in the enclosure, with his little beggar's bag around his neck. It was as if he did not feel the cold. He was barely covered. And he smiled incessantly.

When the chief of the house awoke, they brought him water to wash in preparation for the milking of his favorite cow. Without a second thought the stranger offered a helping hand. Inabwiza's father heartily accepted. His heart had softened under the sway of the foreign man's charm. His daughter observed from afar. Her heart also had undergone a change; it was beating dangerously in her chest... With a thousand precautions, the passerby took the cow's udders, oiled them up, and began to milk. Those shoulders... It was the cow that had been given to her father! She also was called Inabwiza!

"Uwzogomba kumutwara arazompa inyambo isa nk'urya mwamikazi!" "He who wants to take my daughter will give me a cow that resembles this queen!" her father thundered each time he addressed the other fathers pressing him to give up his treasure.

Inabwiza spied on each of the stranger's movements. He had a certain way of milking—fluid, precise, extremely focused. He watched the cow's udder intensely, patted its rump, plunged his hands into the calabash set at his feet to wet his fine, long fingers. He coated them with oil, then began milking again with greater intensity. Two times he touched the little snakeskin bag hung from his neck. One time he sneezed.

"Oooooh! Oohhhhhhh! Ndabira namwe bantu b'Imana!" "For my sake, men of God, look upon this!" Watching the young man, Inabwiza's father gushed. His esteem only increased. It had been decided in his heart for quite some time that he would give his daughter to this man. Now there was a strong temptation to leave him this cow as well... From his left eye fell a tear. A tear of joy. He remembered his wife in her moments of joy. How very beautiful she still was when she had left him.

"Here you go, my father! I have paid tribute to your cows and to your house, for the warm welcome that you reserved for me yesterday," he said when he finished milking Inabwiza. "Now I will continue my journey in peace."

A little pang gripped the old man's heart.

"Would you not stay a few more days? Do you not see that my queen loves you?" Inabwiza's father asked with a false laugh.

"*Ha! Ego muvyeyi muga bagira ngo impinga itagira umugenzi igira ngo ugende bwije... Urwo nararusimvye kuko nasanze umuryango kurugendo!*" "Yes, my father, wisdom says that a traveler without friends should travel by night in foreign regions... I escaped that affliction, for I have found family along my route. "*Mugabo, ntunyibagirire yuko impinga y amperekeza itagenda umwe...*" "But do not forget that wild, open country is not to be traversed alone...allow me to accompany you""*Reka ndahanyonyagire hakibona, ubwo simbura uwo dufatanya urugendo*" "Let me depart as soon as day breaks, I will most assuredly find someone to accompany me along the way."

Inabwiza's father stared at him for a long time. Straight into his eyes. Everyone was there. Then he gave him his second proper spear as a gift—the first one had gone to his eldest son: "*Umushitsi ntatera ubworo buba ari ubwari buhasanzwe.*" "A guest does not bring about poverty; it was there before his arrival," he says to him.

He filled the beggar's bag with smoked meat, gave him two wooden jars filled with curdled milk, and then walked with him for a long while. After the second valley, Inabwiza's father stopped and blessed him. Then he let the stranger continue on his way. The old man had wanted to tell him, far from indiscreet ears: "*Uragaruka kuraba so wawe rutara-mutwara!*" "Return to see your father before death takes him away."

But, as wisdom says so well, *ntawuhisha umwotsi inzu iriko irasha*, it is impossible to hide a burning house's smoke. A rumor spread that Inabwiza had been promised to a stranger… She was coveted all the more intensely. The young men who had grown up with her became especially jealous of the passerby who, with seductive words, had succeeded where all others had failed.

The bids rose, the offers of cows became truly disturbing. But Inabwiza's father thought of it no longer. His daughter was maturing. She saw more and more handsome men in the courtyard, and she showed impressive forbearance as she awaited her momentous wedding. But her father's heart was ever turned towards that spot two valleys away on an uphill slope, where a handshake had sealed an eternal link between father and son-in-law…

One day, when the old man returned home earlier than normal, he found his daughter already lying down in the house's main room. She was sweating. The servants were busy around her. They didn't know what to do—it was the first time that such a thing had occurred.

While the sun was still soaring over the vast family hut, she had left the fields, complaining of a buzzing in her head. Since then, she had been moaning on the mat spread across the room's threshold, so that she could have a little air. Her father felt a great sorrow crashing down upon him.

He kneeled and took his gentle Inabwiza by the hand.

"What do you want, my queen?" he asked her.

"To live!" came the sick girl's reply.

The old father quickly called his *mupfumu*, his seer, and summoned the entire family. The nine brothers were all there that evening, each accompanied by his respective seer. It was a serious matter. The countryside was mobilized, waiting with bated breath for the wise men's diagnoses.

They screamed and they cried and they called upon their ancestors' spirits, and they did many other things, mysterious and unknown to most men. An hour passed. The personal seer of Inabwiza's father was beyond recognition, his eyes rolled back in his head. The word came: Inabwiza was sick because she was alone. "*Irungu riranunuza amaraso yawe.*" "Solitude sucks one's blood," projected the wise man in the direction of the crazed father. In plain language, "marry your daughter off as soon as possible!" the knowing one said.

Otherwise, "the ancestors will reclaim this treasure perishing before our very eyes, this hoe rusting from lack of use, this sterile heifer dying for want of impregnation." This was said by his sons' seers, who joined the great *mupfumu* still shivering from the shock of the terrible encounters they had to undergo in order to receive the oracle.

They justified the word of the ancestral forces by indicating the growing displeasure of the region's young men, all incapable of wresting the most beautiful of women from her father. "This causes useless rivalries between the people. They are ready to steal cows in order to have your daughter, and the other daughters of the region become extremely irritable as soon as her name is mentioned. Mothers see their sons, formerly energetic at work and in good health, grown thin from pining after Inabwiza. They will soon begin to poison themselves," it was communicated to him.

"And who knows if they will not begin with you?" That question made the old man start from fear. So the young man with the snakeskin hanging from his neck would not see him before his death? Were crafty spirits forcing him to give Inabwiza to suitors against his wishes?

"*Ibere ry'uwansize iyo nzogenda ntamuhaye uwo nshaka!*" "May I undress my daughter's breast if I do not give Inabwiza to the man that I choose!" swore the old man in his heart. Around him, people kept talking, his sons with seers and even the neighbors, happy to give a lecture to this stubborn man who was going to kill his daughter from fear of letting her go!

They reminded him even of that ancient saying that pro-
claimed *ugutanga kuzana umugisha kuruta guhabwa*, giving
bestows greater blessings than receiving. But Inabwiza's
father turned a deaf ear.

The night passed. A long, long night.

Day followed day. After his daughter, the father also
fell gravely ill. Because of another infection: the anxiety of not seeing "his son" again, the one who was to
come and say goodbye, to take Inabwiza away before
his death. That was very feasible. She barely spoke anymore. All the great seers of the region had come to visit
her. From his perspective, they preferred to remain quiet for fear of seeming charlatans if they didn't cure her.
What was most worrying was that she kept her beautiful
complexion. When she got up from her bed—rarely, it is
true—they compared her beauty to that of queens in the
Royal Court of Muramvya...

Then one evening, the sick girl's skin still burning hot,
the first cow sneezed. The bull did the same. Inabwiza's
father was weak, but he had to arise because, they said to
him, his daughter urgently wanted to speak to him. "She
is going to leave me," the old father thought. But when he
leaned over the bed of his queen, what he heard filled him
with consternation.

"Tomorrow morning can you milk Inabwiza?" pleaded
Inabwiza.

"What would I not do for my queen?"

Very early the next morning the courtyard was tidied
up. The servants helped the old man get set up under
the swollen udders of his favorite cow. Beforehand, he
had come by to see his daughter who, like most nights of
late, had not slept at all. The features of the most beautiful of daughters were very tense, because... the cows had
sneezed a great deal during the night!

"When you are milking her, touch the rump of Inabwiza two times, then pretend that you are touching the base of her neck," Inabwiza asked of her father.

The father situated himself under the udders of his most beautiful cow—God knows he had many beautiful cows!—and he did exactly as his daughter asked.

That evening, Inabwiza walked in the courtyard. The next day, she welcomed the stranger from before, who returned now with a long retinue of servants and cows to pay the dowry for the most beautiful of daughters. They learned that his name was Kabonero, and he was a prince.

"*Urukundo ruraronderwa*" "Love will try to find itself." were the first words of Kabonero when he tenderly embraced Inabwiza's father. Tears flowed from the old man's eyes. That evening he assembled the two young lovers and blessed them. Then he asked his entire family, assembled in his vast hut, to let out cries of joy. "*Bananje impundu nti-bungwa*" "My children, cries of joy cannot be eaten away by worms"… Those were his last words. The old man had been right to preserve his daughter.

"May the story die, but I remain," the one-eyed woman concluded when she told this story to her grandchildren. Often, they would fall asleep before hearing the end of the story, lulled to sleep by her mellifluous voice. A scene from childhood; an act of wisdom. In any case they knew that the story would end well… They dozed, waking for the length of three or four episodes, and then fell straight asleep. With confidence in the story's ending.

Tales should be prescribed to adults as well. They are an excellent sedative. Except that adults know that the end is not always so nice. And adults are not always lulled to sleep by words.

Here—see for yourselves—this sad scrap that is going to be hung in a little bit! What kind of tale must he be told to still believe that life's stories have nice endings?

She remembers the days when her mother would tell her this story. She was young, very young, back when she loved to play with dirt. She had even asked her mother to teach her to make earthenware. *"Mbe wa mukobwanje, ayo maraso wayakuye he?"* "Tell me, my daughter, whose blood runs in your veins?" she would ask her each time… for at that time it was humiliating to be a "potter". There were, it was said, a category of men who deserved the task. But what she did not understand was that a product of such low origin could occupy such an important role in social life. The *inkono*, pitchers, served to cook the meals and to keep water fresh. These objects were essential.

The one-eyed old woman has respect for every living thing living. From a young age she knew to respect the Twas, the third ethnic group after the Hutus and the Tutsis. It was even murmured that she might be one of them, by her father's bloodlines. But it does not matter! The essential thing is to live.

XI

Kuvuga menshi siko kuyamara
To speak much is not to
exhaust one's words

The mission had been demanding. Channeling Hariho's rage had required a plan of attack.

The leader's first move—one of great urgency—was to join in chanting the rallying cry with the others, "Die! Die!" This made *him* one of them and reduced his liability were the operation to fail.

Then, after having shouted more than the others, *he* hurled himself at Nyamuragi to become the central—or at least the most prominent—force driving the Court's procession. To guide the participants through this session's docket.

What would go first? The shouts of the mob, of course. In that monstrous hubbub, it was easy to say anything or everything, even to maintain total silence while appearing to scream. Two times *he* had made his presence known to Nyamuragi. "*Ntugire ubwoba ntaco uba ariho ndi!*" "Don't be afraid; nothing will happen to you as long as I am here." Of course for this man, who had seen his share of horrific scenes, the very real "something" that could happen to the young mute was "the" thing: death. The rest—blows and insults, large wounds and small, deforming Nyamuragi's body here and there—all that was merely contingent.

Nothing serious. In that moment, the most important thing was to save a life.

As the shouting continued and, in the absence of some authoritative word, it remained unclear what would come next, it was possible for *him* to maneuver in secret. That is to say openly, in full sight of all. Shouts fed on other shouts. The crowd swelled in a slow progression towards the summit of Kanya's hill.

By virtue of a rule in this tight-knit community so abused by fate (it hadn't rained for two months, and this was the rainy season!), when a matter becomes public—or not—it also becomes a personal matter for every self-respecting Harihai. Every man and woman wished to know the reason for the shouting, which only led to even more shouting as each one sought to be heard, thus feeding in volume and intensity the noise reverberating around Kanya's summit.

The mass of thrill-seekers packed together. It grew. Time passed. And all these fine people still did not know the precise reason for their gathering. Thus, there were no less than two hundred pairs of eyes assembled waiting to see an accused man flail at the end of a rope.

The second position in the procession was occupied by the enigmatic leader himself! He had to be near the shouting in order to control it and determine its general trend. It is not easy to stay abreast of what two hundred souls are saying, but it is possible to instill in each of those beings the same thought: the thought of death.

In the third position came the crowd, of course. They had to feel near the theater of operations. They had to live out the events as closely as possible, even as a filter was established between them and the shouts (that is to say, what might take shape from that verbal muddle should more attention be paid). That filter was *him*.

Let's return to the intermediary position, to *his* delicate task. The leader was at once the interpreter of the shouting and the ear scanning the assembly's emotions. Swelling chests, rapid breathing, hands clawing with impatience, sweat tracing channels across faces hungry for blood. All that. All that had to be noted.

He read a bloodthirst on the faces of everyone. Which yielded in short: "*Mwice arakaranduka!*" "Kill him! May he be uprooted!"

It is not easy to stay abreast of what two hundred souls are saying, but it is possible to instill in each of those beings the same thought. *Death!* he repeated to himself.

He had served on the frontlines. He knew that tactical decisions win wars. The disorderly two hundred-strong crowd did not overwhelm him. He knew they were weak. Because he was systematic. And especially because *kuvuga menshi siko kuyamara*—to speak much does not imply exhausting one's words. He had to act.

What mattered most to *him* was the method of execution they would require of the captured defendant. Did they intend to bludgeon him to death? No! He was not a thief. He was worse: a rapist! Could they dispose of him by stoning? Impossible! He would die too quickly. It must not be forgotten that the idea of delivering him to the police had been immediately dismissed: they wouldn't know what to do with him.

A clean and exemplary death was thus necessary, to imprint itself on the hearts of all those present here and to be recounted for generations. Just like that time long ago in the camp, with poor Longin. It was necessary to send a clear message: Rape is a vile act and cannot be allowed to recur. The rope!

Thirty minutes ago, at the beginning of this dramatic adventure, *he* had suggested to his accomplices: *"Reka n'umwana waha abone ko ari ishano, gufata umukobwa ku nguvu!"* "Let's make sure the children of our region know that rape is a blight we will not tolerate in our midst!" Thus he had justified the choice of this sensational torture.

He had even argued: If hung, swaying in the wind at the summit of Kanya's hill—bare except for the immense fig tree standing almost exactly in its center—Nyamuragi's body would be visible from afar. Of all the hills in the region, mothers would lift their faces towards Kanya and say to themselves: There our honor was redeemed!

Small children would thus grow up in the shadow of that fear. For generations to come they would tell the story of this man who dared to sully the history of Hariho and who was hung by its vigilant people!

The fig tree at the summit of Kanya would be a living monument to the people's renewed link with the heavens. Rain would come again.

"Rabe namwe ingene ibiharage vyumiye hagati. N'ibitoke biriko birabenja bihagaze. Mbega ni mwibaze ikintu: ni kubera iki?" "See for yourselves how the young bean plants have dried out in the midst of the growing season. Even the banana trees are going yellow right before our eyes! Ask yourselves a question—why?" the lively man had yelled, his lungs almost bursting.

Sure of the effect of *his* question, sent whirling through the memories of his fellow men and women for several seconds, he continued. Speaking in public... never let others speak, impede them from thinking, confuse them with an avalanche of words—an elementary principle of oratorical jousting applied with honesty in Hariho. So he continued: "*Abantu nk'aba nibo basivya isi, nibo babuza imvura kugwa mu gushavuza Imana. Mu Njili handitse ngo nimba ari ijisho ryawe ryokugwisha, rirokore ugumane rimwe hako umuriro udahera ukuravya ufise yose.*"

The rant was crafty: "Men such as this poison the earth. They are the ones who provoke God and keep the rain from falling! In the Holy Book it is written, if your eye is a source of depravity, then tear it out and remain with a single one, rather than being consumed in the fires of Hell with two!"

"*Hariho umuriro uruta aya mahano urimwo?*" "Is there a greater Hell than the agony that we are currently living?" he asked his captive audience.

Then *he* turned to the thirty-some people surrounding him, whose shadows were cast over Nyamuragi, lying unconscious on the rocky ground. These closest ones would have the responsibility of transmitting the final decision to those further out. For the moment, he had to convince their leader.

"*Oya! Nk'uko ubivuze, dutegerezwa kwikura ico ceyi. Nayo ubundi tuzohona.*" "Of course, as you say, we should dispense with this embarrassment! Otherwise we will all perish," the other leader responded.

Out on the fringes of that human mass, people wondered what was being said in the center. They knew that the monster had fainted. They speculated: "We are waiting for him to wake up, so as not to kill an unconscious man."

The people are wise; they know that justice exists to straighten out consciences, to consecrate the virtue of the just, and to dismiss the consciences of the impure. In action as much as in speech. Nyamuragi's verdict had been pronounced: "Guilty!" Only the punishment remained. They awaited the execution. Patiently.

While waiting, they spoke of the condemned man. They tried to recall the faces of his poor parents carried away by the war. When all was said and done they knew very little about him. One man explained, with powerful twirling of the arms, that previously Nyamuragi's family owned sheep, the only wealth of which they could boast. There was great murmuring. Shouting as well.

"Reka, n'umwana bazomucire umugani!" "Let's make sure that our actions are passed on to future generations!" they decided.

That was everything. All that remained now was to find a hemp rope—a virgin one—to hang the rapist. Volunteers were sent out. Fifteen minutes later, everything was ready. Meanwhile, Nyamuragi had awoken, only to drift back to sleep again.

They had prepared a solid branch and tested its strength, for Nyamuragi's weight was not inconsequential. They knew he was a big eater. *"Urabiruka ivyo wamiraguye ejo, wa gipfu we!"* "You're about to regurgitate what you swallowed yesterday, you monster!" they insulted him.

Nyamuragi no longer moved. He followed what was happening around him from afar—from very far away—now that he had regained his composure. Warm tears ran from his cheeks; widening channels in the dust streamed down his face. A mask. A grotesque mask with blood here, lumps there, reddish lips, a doughy tongue...

They took him by the armpits. They dragged him under the branch. A deafening silence fell on the hill.

All eyes turned towards the man holding the rope. He quickly passed it around the mute's neck. He tied the knot…

A gunshot went off! Total panic. Everyone present scattered. Imagine, the terror of gunfire thundering next to you!

The silence was broken, but this time, by the sound of feet trampling down the slope of Kanya as dozens hurtled to safety. They did not know who had fired or who was firing. But that was to be determined later! Right now they had to run for their lives…

On the hill, a second gunshot went off. *He* still held the rope tied around the convict's neck. But *he* had flattened himself on the ground to be like the others. As for Nyamuragi, he was no longer there, edging towards death. Before the hanging could even begin.

On the other side of the hill, chosen by the People's Court to execute the presumed rapist, there suddenly appeared a squad of six police officers drenched in sweat. *He* had taken the trouble of informing one of his friends, who had called the police. Arriving near Nyamuragi's body, the head of the new delegation bent over, taking the mute's pulse. Feeling weak life beating through the veins of the mute's neck, he ordered his men to pick him up. They grasped him swiftly but cautiously, and hastened to the pickup waiting below.

He followed behind, his heart beginning to find its normal rhythm again. *He* could breathe. And then a small gesture made in the direction of a former brother-in-arms who happened to be present. His assistant during Nyamuragi's trial.

Just a reflexive lifting of two crossed fingers had moved Eric like a spring. He had discreetly withdrawn from the bloodthirsty crowd and called the police. The People's Court had manifestly forgotten that the mobile phone existed…

As for everything else, all that was required for *him* to do was to delay the sentence's execution. He commissioned useless debates. They could have killed Nyamuragi more quickly if they had wanted. In any case, he couldn't kill his nephew, right? There before his own eyes? Nyamuragi was only a child, as everyone in the family knew.

The way Jonathan saw things, no matter what the innocent endure, there is still only one penalty: the life sentence!

When the shots went off, the one-eyed old woman had also fled. Out of prudence. *These Whites had invented so many harmful things… shotguns, for instance! Look how my poor goats jumped when they heard the gunshots! And the rapist, they couldn't even kill him! The people should have kept their composure and hung him, come what may!* she thought, scampering along behind her flock. The perceptive woman had noted all of the ringleader's tricks. His cries of rage, his soaring oratory, his way of noisily calling for witnesses. She had known that something was up all along.

She thought, surely these theatrics were not all necessary to defend the community's purity. But she had not wanted to intercede. To ask, for example, why they were going to the market to find a rope if they wanted to eliminate him as quickly as possible? While they were at it, she thought, they could have taken the defendant and carted him before an actual court of justice, to get an exemplary judgment. Truly, it would have been an easy sentence in light of the misfortune he had endured since this morning. But that was the price to pay. The redemption of his soul required several stages of suffering, the worst of which sometimes… is death. A painful stage, but a necessary one.

What would her father have said if he were still living? And her mother? They would have called for an assembly of wise men, a council of public figures to meet and decide the case. They would not have killed him. Perhaps they would have only exiled him for life.

XII

Umugabo ni uworya utwiwe n'utwabandi

**A true man enjoys his
possessions and those of others**

The movement of a wild beast. Furtive, in a bare savanna. He can reveal himself eventually, but before overtaking his prey, he can never allow his intentions to show. He advances slowly...

Such is the leader of this righteous assembly. And yet the assembly is unaware of the whirring inside his manly chest, the sweat moistening his sturdy back, or his tense toes curled up inside shoes that once were black but now sport a reddish crust of cheap shoe polish. He did everything possible to cover up his true identity: spitting on the killer, earnestly laying into the accused. Earnestly, with fury and dexterity, a series of avocado tree branches swiftly broken on the prostrate man's young back. He hastened to master the situation. He even suggested that the sentence be exemplary, that its execution be memorable, that the rapist be hung high and dry. He bellowed loudly in the midst of that screaming crowd, turning his voice a raspy hue. But it held valiantly, as did his demeanor. He had to play the game.

Mask reality. The leader, "him," "he"—by his rightful name, Jonathan—managed to conceal himself from the members of the People's Court. An irrefutable alibi for the offense that he intends to commit.

They think he is one of their own, the chief who is supposed to execute their judgments. But they are mistaken: it is he who has played them. Jonathan has managed to control the crowd. Usually, a criminal caught in the act by an angered multitude gets himself lynched.

Aided by his hunter's instinct in the dusty free-for-all this morning, Jonathan has manipulated the beast—that beast with two hundred heads and just as many pairs of arms—and kept them from grabbing rocks to stone Nyamuragi to death.

Jonathan knows something about violence—he is a demobilized soldier. He knows where to apply pressure in order to produce cries of pain, and he knows how to strike an enemy to put him to sleep. Momentarily or forever. Except that Nyamuragi is not an enemy. He is Jonathan's nephew.

Connected to a paternal aunt via a series of more or less smart marriages dating from the time of his great-grandfather, Jonathan's brother was able to take up residence with the aunt when he moved to the province of Karusi (the birthplace of the mute's mother, whose cousin he later took as a wife). Uncle by marriage—a link to be made use of judiciously. It is said, "*uwawe umubonera mu makuba*," we only discover our kin in difficult circumstances.

The most difficult circumstance he ever experienced was during wartime, when it was to kill or be killed. At the time of The Situation.

In the beginning, it was a tale of treason. For every army has its spies, every regiment its traitors. It is the law of nature. A young man promptly bribed (the details were only learned after his death), who then began to supply the enemy with that precious commodity needed for such enterprises to function: information. He reported to the enemy his unit's movements and troop morale. This lasted three weeks and five days, plus the one day he went into the city for what he described to his lieutenant as a "holiday outing." He enjoyed this period because of certain monetary benefits. How much was never precisely determined. But the evil had been committed. It became known as The Situation, a serious and consequently tragic affair.

In the beginning, it was nothing more than a transaction involving military intelligence to the benefit of the opposing army. But the most disturbing thing about these kinds of situations is that the beginning often corresponds with the end. To betray the men whose destiny you are supposed to share, and with whom you are risking everything under the same monstrous shadow—the shadow of death... In truth, it was an enormous transgression. And to top it all off, this traitor had also belittled his own unit, describing them to the enemy as "an assembly of cowards and lecherous men..."

No! In all seriousness, he had gone too far. If he had at least stuck with reporting his brothers' movements, then they doubtlessly would have reacted to the affront with more restraint. But to call them cowards—the very men who had abandoned their own to go to the front, young men who had chosen to trust in Providence rather than hide away in juvenile home life—well, that was the last straw.

When the traitor returned to camp that evening, smelling strongly of hops, they wisely allowed him to fall asleep inside his shabby green tent. The barefaced traitor even took the liberty of snoring!

An excellent idea, even if he didn't know it, because what came next was nothing more than a succession of groans. When morning arrived, they woke him, gently for a little while longer, and took him to the center of camp.

Colonel B.H. appeared, authoritative and strapping in his senior officer stripes, and began listing the professional mistakes of the drowsy man seated below him. As the higher-ranking man spoke, the traitor gradually roused himself. The list of the miscreant's offenses was extremely long. The principle accusations consisted of two grievances: betrayal of his brothers and bad faith. Indeed, the list was long! The punishment would have to be long and slow as well, and the task would fall to his offended brothers. As is fitting.

So they took the man—no longer one of their own—and tied his hands behind him. They made him sit on the ground without a blow or an insult. Just business between men in respectful silence. The score would be settled as per the established rules of courtesy among comrades. The man seated on the clay soil had lost his wager. Now he would pay. And he would be quiet about it.

Of course, to order 120 war-hardened men and professional killers to beat a single man would have been catastrophic. In his great wisdom, Colonel B.H. understood this, which is why he delegated three emissaries with the highly diplomatic task of forcing the man to pay tribute to this corps that was now dead to him. Jonathan, the uncle of Nyamuragi, was among the diplomats dispatched to the central grounds of the twenty-tent encampment.

After the customary preliminary obligations—firmly binding his feet in such a way that he could not stand back up, and tying him firmly to a stake anchored in the fertile soil—they then brought out the wood.

The logs were solid, thick, and well dried. The camp kitchens had not caused any problems for the three emissaries, because they had been granted special powers of requisition in order to bring their critical mission to fruition with as little delay as possible.

The traitor then began to scream. It was a strange noise in the silent camp. No one spoke; the honor guard, standing at attention, watched unflappably. Noise had been formally discouraged by Colonel B.H. "This affair demands the greatest of discretion!" he had murmured to himself. And so it was, remarkably: twenty-four men observed it in utter silence. In fact, it was the first time that such an affair had occurred among them. Outside, another thirty-nine armed men kept the encampment under watch, set off in separate posts of five or seven per patrol.

The long howls continued, interspersed with groans against a horizon that loomed darkly! Cries for his mother. Cries for the clemency of his companions-in-arms observing him here. Reminders of shared episodes of blood and guts and of armed feats they had accomplished together. And, of course, reminders of his brothers and sisters. Feeling death approach the camp like a cold breath on his neck, the living-dead seated on the ground began to protest that he was no more. The man asked for death before the torture could begin. The three emissaries, however, were still busy at work, confident that their target was still quite alive. The proof? He was moaning, which was a bad sign. For moaning shows that one is... a coward!

After having disposed of five piles of logs around the screaming man (later they were rapturous about the resistance of his vocal cords), they lit the fire. The wood was so close that the town crier felt the fire bite, but not close enough to immediately char his skin. Jonathan slowly put the torch to the dry brush, successively igniting five glimmering logs. The cabal had begun: the demon began to roast the man.

The one-eyed old woman had nevertheless felt it was all an act. Usually, such anger led to swift action. Frankly, she told herself, if what happened before her eyes was not acting, then they would have killed Nyamuragi as soon as he was captured. The more the jurors got lost in negotiations and discussions, the more they risked a lighter sentence. The jurors should have stood as one to decide on a punishment. That would have been healthier, for the respect of those presiding, for the defendants, and for the mass of people following this affair closely. There were plenty of stones to kill him quickly if they had really wanted to. But instead they had prattled on. Oh whatever! In any case, what had to happen would happen.

The goats were still chewing away. They were calmer. Their little rounded-out bellies of black fur gleamed under the hot sun.

The old woman never perspired. She only drank water every third day. But she did drink a bowl of banana wine every six hours. She ate twice a day, around eleven and then at seven in the evening. In matters of taste, she was fond of the *intore*, bitter prunes, as well as cassava dough combined with black beans drowned in a fry sauce. She didn't chew tobacco often; she still had virtually all her teeth. Which is a good sign. Her oldest son lived in a house he had built twenty or so meters from his father's.

The one-eyed woman's only granddaughter from her first child came every day to draw water for her and to sweep the main room of her little house (which had only three rooms) before going home. In the mornings, the one-eyed woman ate something light, either bean leaves coupled with a sweet potato or bread when she felt like it, completed by a tomato that she dusted with salt (she had seen it done for the first time by her youngest daughter recently returned from Bujumbura). One hour later, she had her *urwarwa*, the bowl of banana wine.

Every Saturday, she went to the refreshment stand down the paved road from her home for her customary bottle of hot Primus. It had been a tradition since the time of her dearly departed husband, when they would go together. Sometimes her husband would buy her a skewer of grilled goat, but she never had more than one per month. The rest of the time she would weave beautiful wicker baskets, which she sold in the market or gave to her second son who would sell them and bring her back the money. The old woman got on well. "*Ubuzima ni bukebuke*," she loved to say. "Life is slowly."

The heat was there, close by, all-consuming. A dreadful aroma of roasted human flesh floated over the camp after four and a half hours of Longin's inhuman cries. That was the traitor's name. The air was heavy with a diffuse heat, along with Longin's screams of pain and the dark thoughts of his comrades watching him suffer. An unhealthy humidity resulted. Some men had broken ranks and were busying themselves in their bivouacs. Others were cleaning and polishing their rifles. Still others were sleeping or conversing. A dissatisfied or curious man would occasionally rise or return, like the fifteen-year-old in well-folded combat pants who came back at least three times to contemplate the torture. The sight was really quite awful. A heart thundered in each man. Secretly. But that's what Colonel B.H. had wanted.

Hands tied behind his back, Longin whirled and whirled around the stake trying to escape the steady bite of the fire. Which roasted him all the more. After four hours in hell, his skin had become so tender that a baby's scratch could have scraped it off. Longin tried to get up, shaking everything, shuddering, crying, roaring, pleading, and begging forgiveness, but the stake held strong; the ropes resisted still. He continued to roast.

Six hours later, he had calmed down. His hindquarters were covered in blood and his body had begun to coil around his feet. Then his skin began to let out pus, with large lumps full of clear liquid. After 14:30, no one came near the pyre. The odor was that horrifying.

At 15:30, Longin began the funeral oration. He spoke of everything: of his life of poverty and his passion for weapons since he was eleven. He recounted the first time he had played soccer. He described his love for Primus beer in detail and gave reasons (oh, it was so good!) He even managed to slip in an insult against those angels of Satan who were slowly killing him with low heat. He bargained with Jesus to get into heaven, and seeing as how he had time on the pyre to make a confession, he recounted how the previous day he had made a poor sum for his services as a informer (with respect to the current going price). He recalled the love that he had sworn to Yolande, his young flame, and he reminded them of a missive that would need to be passed on to her. He described the father he had never known. He asked for water to drink, and then he fell silent. All of which took about an hour and thirty minutes.

At 17:00 Longin, who had lived the life of a human, died the death of an animal. Cooked like a poor chicken. Death opened wide its mouth to swallow the roast.

The three emissaries returned for their last respects. They put out the faithful logs that were still burning, and then they untied the corpse. Longin's corpse was dropped on top of a brand new mat. Slimy and with an unbearable stench, it was carried by an honor guard of his former comrades. He was buried at 17:43. By 18:00, everything had returned to normal. Except the hearts of a hundred and nineteen men.

This morning, Jonathan had just left the market when he heard the cries of those pursuing his nephew. He quickly went to see, fortunately as it turned out.

When he arrived at the site where Nyamuragi had been captured, the image of Longin was imprinted upon his mind: a man at the heart of a storm… who was about to be devoured. "No, no, no!" beat his heart. Jonathan knew his nephew well. Nyamuragi's mother had sometimes spoken of him in such affectionate tones that he could not believe for an instant that Nyamuragi had been able to attack a young girl!

Alas! The people had made a mistake this time, Jonathan thought. He had to act with the same urgency required to execute Colonel B.H.'s orders in service of a cause deemed appropriate and just. He had to act fast to save his nephew from the claws of the angry mob.

But such a thing was no small matter. Indeed, the rabble's claws were insatiable. Mob rule knows no reverence. As seen during Longin's fiery execution. Reverence, cadence, restraint, and contained severity are what make a good court. These are the things that draw us to goodness and make Justice just. It is not loud. It is ordered and meticulous. Like that other time. In the camp.

For all the reasons mentioned above and out of respect for the principles he had always found necessary for his own good health, notably charity (because *ukora ineza ikaguherekeza*, the good you've done follows you)—Jonathan decided to apply another sentence: he granted Nyamuragi his life.

XIII

Amagara ni amazi aseseka ntibayore
**Life is like water that spills onto the earth,
never to be gathered together again**

Decorum is everything, the intrepid woman tells herself. Her goats graze and graze... Hanging, lynching, imprisonment, exile for life: all these are mere judgments. Sanctions that can never manage to compensate for a victim's pain, she concludes. Her left gum itches occasionally. She throws away a wisp of straw that she has been chewing on, takes a corner of her loincloth and unties it to dig out a little plug of tobacco, cautiously places the precious commodity in the right corner of her reeking mouth—even she knows that it reeks—and then closes her mouth. Passersby greet her; she smiles and grumbles a *mahoro* in return. Then with the end of her staff she nudges the lean rump of one of her goats away from the cassava leaves it had been heading for. She ties her headscarf just tight enough and then sneezes. Disturbances mark our entire life, whichever way you look at it. The most important thing is to disturb life itself without letting it fall to pieces. Life is the water that flows over the earth, never to be gathered together again... the one-eyed old woman reflects as she continues on her way.

TRANSLATOR'S NOTE

There is an omission at the heart of *Baho!* that may surprise a reader familiar with postcolonial Burundian history. Like its better known neighbor Rwanda, Burundi has been haunted by ethnic conflict between the majority Hutus, who traditionally compose the lower socioeconomic classes, and the minority but traditionally higher class Tutsis. This ethnic conflict has repeatedly descended into violence. In its half century of existence, Burundi has endured more than five coups d'etat, a king's assassination, two presidential assassinations, and three periods of massive bloodletting, two of which are often labelled as genocides. Yet, in Rugero's novel, we never learn the ethnicity of the unfairly accused Nyamuragi, his uncle Jonathan, or the nameless one-eyed old woman, to say nothing of the more minor characters. The words "Hutu" and "Tutsi" appear only once in fact, and then only to define the country's third ethnic group, the Twa. Ethnic conflict—one of the defining characteristics of Burundi's short postcolonial history—is absent from *Baho!*

The single passage in Rugero's novel where the subject of ethnicity is broached appears at the end of Chapter 10:

> The one-eyed old woman has respect for every living thing. From a young age she knew to respect the Twas, the third ethnic group after the Hutus and the Tutsis. It was even murmured that she might be one of them, by her father's bloodlines. But it does not matter! The essential thing is to live.

In discussions about ethnic conflict in the Great Lakes region, the Twas are often forgotten. The region's indigenous population, formerly known as pygmies—a term they now reject for its negative implications—comprise 1% of Burundi's population. Traditionally, they were nomadic hunters who traded meat for agricultural products with sedentary Bantu peoples like the Hutus and Tutsis. Having been forced out of their nomadic ways, the Twas now constitute the lowest rung of Burundi's caste system, marginalized by most Tutsis and Hutus, and often even considered subhuman. The pensive old woman's attitude thus provides a powerful counterpoint to commonly held views about the Twas in Burundian society. While the novel does not address Hutu-Tutsi tensions, its single mention of ethnicity does propose a position of radical ethnic harmony. The old woman shares the wisdom of her years: all lives are to be valued, not just those of one ethnicity. Then, as quickly as the subject of ethnicity is raised, it is dropped and the narrative moves on.

We see other hints of this radical inclusivism when Nyamuragi's father criticizes European schools:

> "The White Man's School is disrespectful of human life. It should welcome all who desire to study and educate them according to their abilities! Why does it choose which ones will come to fruition? Why does it not dedicate itself to all the seeds presented to it by the people? Why does the White Man's School select those who are normal, and not you, my child? The strong, the intelligent, those who know how to speak..."

Whether it is the Burundian caste system or views on the disabled, there is a strong universalist critique at work within Rugero's novel. In contrast with the reality of so much human history, in Burundi and elsewhere, characters at key moments in *Baho!* tell us that all life should be accepted, cultivated, and loved.

At times this emphasis on loving existence verges on the epicurean. Burundians come together to enjoy life when they chatter around a gourd of swirling banana wine, tell stories around the night fire, or dance in nightclubs. Nyamuragi himself loves socializing despite his inability to communicate, and he particularly loves food, as we see in the lavish descriptions of savory Burundian dishes. In such passages, Rugero often employs the word *artiste* to refer to those who revel in these epicurean pleasures of Burundian life. Nyamuragi is an *artiste* when it comes to eating. Mugabo, the man who temporarily breaks up Nyamuragi's mob trial with his roving hands, is an *artiste* in his appreciation for the finer sex. In my translation, I have chosen to render *artiste* as "connoisseur." Although it diminishes the idea of refinement, I believe that it does a better job of capturing the sense of cultivated pleasure that Rugero's *artistes* derive from the simple things in life. In the case of the old woman, the pleasures are more subdued, but, they are there nonetheless. It is not important if one is Hutu, Tutsi, or Twa; the essential thing is to live. To live a life of simple pleasures widely shared.

Burundi is one of the very few countries whose post-colonial borders roughly parallel those of a precolonial political entity, an independent kingdom that ruled for over 200 years before the arrival of Europeans. It has thus been saved the kinds of conflict that plague so much of the postcolonial world. However, like other former colonial states, Burundi's current strife owes much to European colonial policy. After Belgium took over the colony from Germany following World War I, every Burundian was assigned an ethnic identity based on racial theories in vogue at the time. Believing the Tutsis to have descended from tribes more closely related to Europeans that eventually migrated south to the Great Lakes region, those with longer noses and longer necks and owning more cows (10 being the cut-off point) were determined to be Tutsi. According to this theory, Hutus were indigenous to the area and could be identified by their shorter necks, shorter noses, and fewer cows.

The presence of the French language in Burundi predates the Belgians. Beginning during the abbreviated German colonial period, French-speaking Catholic missionaries established a presence throughout the Great Lakes region. Known as the "White Fathers," they are both the greatest source of information about traditional Burundian culture and language and the reason why Christianity and the French language took root in Burundi. From Rugero's choice of language to his allusions to Perrault's fairy tales, *Baho!* never would have been possible without these "White Fathers." While Burundians are Francophone due to their colonial history, their mother tongue is Kirundi, a Bantu language very closely related to the official language of Rwanda, Kinyarwanda. In sprinkling Kirundi passages throughout the French text, both in the proverbs that serve as epigraphs for each chapter and in key moments of dialogue, Rugero continues a well-established tradition in Burundi's Francophone literature.

In 1966, four years after Burundi gained its independence from Belgium, the monarchy was overthrown after refusing to recognize elections won by Hutu candidates. The last King of Burundi was assassinated six years later when he tried to return to the country. Each of the first three presidents were Tutsi military officers who came to power in a coup d'etat. During this time of one-party rule, tensions broke into violence twice, in 1972 and in 1988. The worst violence, however, came after free elections were finally held in 1993. Melchior Ndadaye, elected the first Hutu President, was bayoneted to death a few months after taking office. Then, a year later, President Cyprien Ntaryamira, was assassinated when his airplane was shot down in the same crash that killed Rwandan President Juvénal Habyarimana and triggered the Rwandan Genocide. Burundi's genocide was less deadly than Rwanda's, but its war lasted longer. It effectively destroyed a budding interethnic movement of educated Hutus and Tutsis. Hundreds of thousands were killed. Even more were displaced. Rugero's own family, for instance, left Burundi to take refuge in neighboring Tanzania. In 2000, a peace agreement was ratified, and, in 2005 the rebel Hutu military commander Pierre Nkurunziza was elected President. Since Nkurunziza's 2015 constitutionally controversial decision to seek a third term, Burundi has been wracked by protests, reprisals, and even a failed coup attempt.

Baho! takes place in the wake of that 1993 - 2005 war. In the novel, the residents of the fictional region of Kanya are on edge. Memories of the war occupy their minds, rumors of rape haunt the hills, and a drought drags on. In a narrative that lends itself strongly to Rene Girard's thesis that mimetic desire leads to violence, Nyamuragi becomes a scapegoat for the entire region. The defenseless mute is the perfect object of wrath for a people "overheated with anger and thirsty for rain." The mob leader rants, "Eliminate the impure man and you protect yourself from evil." This language used to denounce him is a language of purity and collective guilt. It elevates his act to much more than attempted rape. And the proposed punishment, lynching with a virgin rope on a hill where all can see, takes on a sacred aura. Nyamuragi becomes both the source of evil in Kanya's midst, and, in his imminent death, redemption from drought and violence. Like the Christ on Good Friday, the ultimate scapegoat in Girard's theory, Nyamuragi is dragged up a hill as a sacrifice for sins he did not commit.

And yet this scapegoating is peculiar. Nyamuragi is innocent of the crime. He did not rape poor Kige; it was clearly a misunderstanding. It is true, scapegoats are innocent more often than not. The true peculiarity is that his very own uncle is the one riling up the mob and demanding his death. Jonathan, who has known Nyamuragi's innocent character since he was a boy, whips the crowd into a frenzy with talk of ritual purity and collective guilt. He pushes the collectivist rhetoric of vengeance to its limits. However, in an ironic reversal, we discover that he is doing so in order to deceive the crowd. He wishes to draw out the workings of mob vengeance in order to undermine them. Thanks to these delay tactics, Nyamuragi ultimately escapes when the police arrive to break up the mob. Here we have another insight into Rugero's vision of Burundi. Despite the rhetoric of inclusivism we find throughout the novel, the reality is that such values are not universally shared. Times are hard, and spontaneous violence is always a possibility. In a country where genocide is a recent memory and where the thirst for vengeance is strong, the will of the people requires not expression, but restraint. One man can channel a mob's anger for only so long. In the end, it requires a greater force to rescue an innocent victim. The police, the most visible part of the state bureaucratic apparatus, arrive to provide justice. The message seems to be: justice can only occur within the constraints of a modern state. A modern state that, we might hope, is as blind to ethnicity as *Baho!* is.

In my translation of *Baho!* I have striven to reflect the influences visible in Rugero's original: traditional French literature, the Bible, and Burundian oral tales and proverbs. The nature of the English language required leveling out elevated French diction, as well as massaging both tenses and typography. I have also smoothed out the sentence flow, joining fragments and chopping up what we would consider run-on sentences. But as much as possible I have hewed to a more literal translation of Rugero's original. My hope is that I have still preserved Rugero's sparse and poetic lyricism.

Gratitude is due those who have helped shepherd my first translation of a novel to publication. First and foremost, David Shook, my extremely patient editor and talented collaborator in words. In so many ways, he made this translation a reality. Brian Hewes was a champion of my translation from the very beginning. Laetitia Citroen, Yann Rousselot, and Abigail Mallin all read over my translation at various points and provided helpful suggestions. And, finally, Zinzi Clemmons provided the last push towards excellence with her astute copy editing. Many thanks to each and every one of you.

I also thank the author, Roland Rugero, for his crucial answers and thoughtful comments. The novel's point of view proved to be particularly tricky at times. Confused about the constantly shifting point of view in one passage, I asked him whether he was attempting to capture the orality of Burundian tales. He confirmed my suspicion, but he also added that Burundians will often overwhelm their conversation partners with a verbal barrage of sometimes contradictory information. It is so common, in fact, that there is a proverb describing this Burundian tendency: *Ijambo rigukunze ni irikugumye mu nda*, "the word you love is the one that finally comes to rest in your belly." As you read *Baho!* my hope is that

Born in 1986 in Burundi, **Roland Rugero** grew up in a family where reading was a favorite pastime. He has worked as a journalist in Burundi since 2008. His novels include Les *Oniriques* and *Baho!*, the first Burundian novel to be translated into English. Rugero has held residencies at La Rochelle and at Iowa's prestigious International Writing Program. In addition to his work as a writer, in 2011 he wrote and directed *Les pieds et les mains*, the second-ever feature-length film from Burundi. Rugero is active in promoting Burundi's literary culture, co-founding the Samandari Workshop and helping found the Michel Kayoza and Andika Prizes. He lives in Bujumbura, Burundi.

Christopher Schaefer is a translator from the Spanish and French living in Paris. He has won the Ezra Pound Award for Best Translation from the University of Pennsylvania for his translations of the Cuban poet Javier Marimón. In 2012 he participated in the English PEN Translation Slam at the Poetry Parnassus in London. He lives in Paris.